Things You Don't Know About Night

The first book

written by Patrick G. Mercado
illustrated by Giorgio Bacchin

A special thanks for those who made this book possible, including:

Editor: Malory Wood of The Missing Ink
Book Designer: Niki Merrett of Merrett Design Ltd.
Ellie and Beehive Illustrations, Ltd
Illustrator: Giorgio Bacchin
My family and friends
And of course, God and Saint Therese

For
Theo and Lilly

Is it something you see
Is it something you hear
Is it not quite clear, this thing, called Night
Is it here to scare
Or help you to dream
It's not what it seems, this is Night

Part I

The Windows in the Sky

This particular story about Night speaks about a love that was lost. Lost mostly due to unbelief. Or perhaps it was forgetting how one ought to believe. To explain how such a thing could be possible, it might be best to begin later in this story, at the part that involves the girl. She was from a small place that she sometimes tried to believe was bigger than it actually was.

She, Nicole, that is, was nine-years-old in 1992 when it all happened. She was rather plain-looking, that is as far as nine-year-old girls go. The clothes she would normally wear didn't make any particular statement except for the days when her attire didn't exactly go together. She was once seen wearing green, plaid pants along with a top that had orange polka dots! And another detail that made people not quite sure what to make of Nicole, were the glasses she chose to wear. They were thick and clunky which often made her look years older.

At the beginning of this story, Nicole was standing in an office that was surely larger than it felt to her then. She found enough space near a window amongst piles of old newspapers and magazines and boxes (some opened, some not). In her hands she held a journal that had the words on its cover, *A Little Bit About Night, By Marc Alexander*. It was a maroon color and had a simple appearance, medium in size. What follows is the passage she happened to be reading at that moment:

There are Windows in the Sky that Night sometimes looks out of. They're these Grand Windows, like the kind you see at those fancy ballrooms but are much too big or cost too much to bring home. Now a window isn't of much use if you can't see what's happening on the other side. Through the Windows in the Sky, Night can see so many things. Naturally, it's hard for us to see those windows from down here… even if we were to pretend.

Nicole looked out the window into the star-filled sky, closed her eyes for a moment, and thought really hard.

… She opened them again. No Windows in the Sky.

"Nicole, Nicole. Remember, that's just make believe, pretend, yes? We wouldn't want people calling you a loon like your father now, would we?" remarked Charles, a short man with round features as he entered the office where Nicole was. If he hadn't such an unfriendly manner about him, Nicole might have thought of him as the cuddly sort, almost like a bear that could be won at a carnival.

"My daddy's not a loon!" Nicole snapped back.

And then without even a mere glance, this man, Charles, made his way past Nicole to have a seat behind a desk that had on it a pile of paper, a coffee cup with the initials "HC" on it, and exactly eight books. He slid the top piece of paper off and as he wrote he spoke to Nicole. "Do you know what they do with crazy people, hmmm? They lock them up in these small rooms where it's dark and their only friends are mice and spiders."

"My Daddy's not crazy. Besides, he said that 'All children have the right to believe in fairy tales if they want to.'"

"Now that doesn't seem too practical," Charles returned. "Nicole, please do try to be quiet until I finish this last form so we can be on our way."

After a quick sip of his coffee, it was back to his paperwork. It was Charles' task to see to it that Nicole's well being was taken care of now that her mother had passed away, and while her father was resting at a place where people are often kept when they are considered"loons".

The time had come when it was decided that Nicole would stay with her Auntie Ruth for the time being. The next train would be leaving that night.

)))) ● ((((

Chug a Chug a Chug a Chug a...The rhythmic sound of the train was mostly soothing during the trip. Even the occasional whistle wasn't enough to cause a major disturbance as everyone in the car appeared to be asleep. The train was nearly dark. One of the lights left on was being used by Nicole as she read from her father's journal. A brief moment passed before she tugged on Charles' arm.

"Mister, Mister Charles?" whispered Nicole.

"Huh, Huh...Wha? Oh, it's you," Charles responded with a yawn.

"Who's Alison?"

"Who?" asked Charles.

Nicole pointed at a page in the journal. "There."

Charles squinted and took a closer look at the page. "Oh, that Alison." He turned his back to her and closed his eyes. "I wouldn't worry about that now, Nicole. This Alison was just part of your father's story. No one's ever met her. No pictures of her to be found. It's just a story. That's all…"

Charles was soon back to sleep… or if he was pretending to be asleep just to avoid answering any more of Nicole's questions, he was quite skillful at it. Nicole took a determined breath and focused on her father's journal once more. This time she read:

Behind the Window in the Sky, in another place, lives a lady named Alison. She is Night herself, or part of those who make up Night. Alison is very pretty and has hazel eyes which are almost brown like her hair.

She wears a blue dress that is as bright as a new day. Sometimes it's green, or gold, or white, or red - But never black. Alison pictures this is how the day looks like when the sun is shining.

When Nicole's eyes turned back up, she saw a woman wearing a blue dress, sitting a few rows ahead. It wasn't a dazzling kind of blue like something Night would wear but it was blue, nonetheless. Maybe in the dim lighting of the train car it looked different.

And then the woman stood up and turned around. Could this be Alison? Nicole thought as she sat up in her seat. She could almost see her face…

"Snort. Hhhchkkk…" were the sounds coming from Charles as he tried to get something out from his throat. He then smacked his lips. Now there was no way Nicole could pretend not to hear these sounds. She had to look his way. Charles' words from earlier came to mind. *Nicole, Nicole. Remember, that's just make believe. Pretend, yes?*

Nicole shook her head and noticed that the woman dressed in blue was back in her seat fast asleep. That's when she realized that it wasn't really Alison, but just her imagination. After closing the journal and putting it in her backpack, Nicole turned her back to Charles and closed her eyes.

)))) ● ((((

The morning they arrived at Auntie Ruth's house, it was bright, a bit warmer than it should be for that time of the day but certainly not enough for Nicole to complain.

"Welcome, Nicole. Come on in!" Auntie Ruth spoke in a soft voice. Nicole had met her Auntie Ruth several times but only once or twice was she old enough to remember. Ruth was a different sort. She was a woman nearly fifty. Her long, curly hair that hung down over her face left room for one to look into her starry eyes (a common thing for artists, which she happened to be.) She seemed like the shy, silent type. Most likely the kind that doesn't receive many guests nor is apt to make many visits that would cause her to travel a lengthy distance. Auntie Ruth just nodded at

Charles as he gave her instructions and paperwork, rarely making eye contact, even as he was leaving them.

The house Auntie Ruth lived in was old. It was a three story, red-brick house with a gray trim that was worn and chipped from the years. The flaws and scratches were made more noticeable now that the sun was shining on the house. Nicole thought that it looked like it could be in one of those creepy, old movies. The ones where there were ghosts inside.

"Ghosts! In here?" Auntie Ruth exclaimed as she looked around the house. "No, there shouldn't be. I thought I had a sign out in front that says 'No Ghosts Allowed in Here!'"

Nicole shook her head.

"There isn't? Well, there should be," Auntie Ruth chuckled. She would have gone on about the topic of ghosts in her house had she not seen the suitcase in Nicole's hand and how weary the girl looked. "We'll have to take care of that later. Now, why don't we get you settled in."

There was a room on the third floor, about 12 feet by 12 feet. It was painted white and was bare except for a lamp, bed, desk and dresser. This is where Nicole set down her suitcase and whatever little else she was able to bring with her.

"And right below you," Auntie Ruth said as she stomped her foot, "is my studio. Do you like to paint, Nicole?" A slight smile found its way onto Nicole's face. "Well, I've got tons and tons of paint and chalk you can use! Maybe you could do something to decorate this room. I left it empty for you."

Once she had rested a bit, Nicole decided that the first thing she would paint would be night. It began as all paintings begin -- with a blank canvas. This would prove harder than she imagined. She didn't know where to start or even what the picture should look like. It wasn't because Nicole had forgotten what night looked like but it was day and it was far too distracting for her. So Nicole thought that she might take a walk first and wait until night time to get a more accurate feel for her painting.

Nicole was more than half way down the sidewalk when Auntie Ruth called out to her, "Now, did you remember my phone number?"

"Yes," Nicole answered as she turned back.

"Okay, and the address here?"

"1375 West Center," was Nicole's second anwer.

After an almost lenghty discussion to make sure that Nicole knew where she was and how she was to get back to this place, she said goodbye to her aunt. Nicole then ventured out to discover her new world. She walked up one street and then to another, and followed by another street... This seemed to go on for quite some time. As Nicole walked on and saw more places, she felt something peculiar. The children in this neighborhood were scarce, if any. Except for Ricky and his friends.

Ricky, as Nicole would find out, was the 14-year-old boy who lived in the house next door to Auntie Ruth. At the time Nicole passed by the place where he lived, Ricky and the other boys were doing nothing in particular. At least, that was how it appeared to Nicole. She thought it was as good a time as any to introduce herself.

"Hello, my name is Nicole. I --- I'm staying with my Auntie Ruth next door for a while... Is this your house?"

The others pointed to Ricky, waiting for his answer. But did he answer her? No! Instead, Ricky sharply turned to one of his friends and as if Nicole hadn't stopped by at all, he muttered.

"So anyway, what were you talking about when ---"

"Excuse me," Nicole spoke up.

"Dude, I think she wants to be your friend," one of the boys said with a smirk.

Ricky got up and with a sigh that turned into an uncaring yawn. He moved towards Nicole. He was looking somewhere else when he responded to her. "Yeah, yeah. You moved in next door. I heard ya. What do you want me to do? Blow a horn? Throw a party?"

Now some might call Ricky the cutest boy in his class but Nicole thought him as very rude. To be somewhat fair to Ricky, he didn't feel it to his advantage for a 14-year-old boy of his stature to be seen with a nine-year-old girl, particularly one who appeared as odd as Nicole.

The dinner Auntie Ruth prepared on the first night Nicole stayed with her, consisted of thinly sliced roast beef along with mushrooms and carrots. The gravy she poured over the meal had a hint of garlic and rosemary.

"I must've seen a million houses and there were no kids to talk to..." Nicole sighed as Auntie Ruth served the dinner onto her plate.

"None?" Auntie Ruth questioned.

"Well, there was the boy next door."

"You mean Ricky. Good kid," Auntie Ruth said as she had a seat.

"I thought he was very rude," Nicole responded.

"Now Nicole," Auntie Ruth said with an understanding voice. "I've known Ricky since he was much younger than you are now. He thinks he's changed. Believe me, he hasn't changed. Give him some time. He's not nearly as rude as he acts these days."

"Still, I don't think I want him as a friend."

"It was just your first day here. Don't worry. I'll tell you what, I'll take you to this park just to prove to you that there's some other kids within 100 miles of here. And when school starts ---"

"I wish I had a friend like Alison," Nicole said as she looked up.

"Alison?" Auntie Ruth spoke. Her eyes looked as if something just came to her. "I remember your father mentioning that name that last time we talked. He said she was from this Night place. Is she the Alison you're talking about?"

"Yes. The one behind the Windows in the Sky. I think she would be very nice."

"I'm sure she is," Auntie Ruth said with a smile.

"I bet if I can find Alison, she can help me get Daddy back," Nicole expressed.

Auntie Ruth thought for a moment and then she said,"Your father told me about her and about Night. It sounded so real. I thought it would be a wonderful thing to believe in ---"

"You believe in Night Auntie Ruth, don't you?"

Auntie Ruth saw the innocence on Nicole's face. "Yes. Yes I do, Nicole." Nicole nodded and began to eat. But before Auntie Ruth joined her, she grabbed the serving ladle and shook it in the air. "And your father's not crazy!"

)))) ● ((((

There are Windows in the Sky that Night sometimes looks out of... was a line that Nicole's father once wrote. In one of her paintings, Nicole attempted to paint a window in her night sky but it appeared more like a black box than what one would think a window looks like. It was because she had painted the sky so dark (which it should be at nighttime) that the window could barely be seen.

Nicole thought she could fix this in her next picture by starting with the window first and then painting the night sky around it. Once she painted the window, she added a beautiful woman behind it looking out. This most likely would be Alison.

After this painting was finished, it wasn't exactly what Nicole had expected. The window didn't look quite right up there in the sky at night. It wasn't a natural thing but what was more important is now Nicole could see the window. This would do good to help her in what she had planned to do next.

Alison

It was on a Thursday when Nicole first attempted to call on Night in hopes that Alison would come down. Needless to say she had no idea of the proper procedure for such an undertaking. If only her father was there to nudge her along, or at least show her where the best place to start was. But all Nicole had at this time was her father's journal. This would have to do.

On the edge of Auntie Ruth's back porch sat Nicole. After reading a few lines from the journal, she mouthed a few words, looking like she was trying to remember something.

Nicole set the journal down on the porch and moved into the back lawn. She stretched out her arms and began to sing a song. The song was about Night. It was hardly in tune and the words didn't always rhyme but it was the song Nicole sang and it came from her heart.

In the yard next door was a large tree. In that tree was a treehouse where two boys hung out. One of the boys was Ricky, and Andrew was the name of the other. Andrew stopped reading his comic book and lifted his head when Nicole's song faintly reached his ears as they sat up in the treehouse.

"What the…" Andrew mumbled.

He climbed down from where he sat, and moved towards the fence. There was a crack in the fence that was large enough for Andrew to peek through. And what he saw on the other side made him laugh. There he saw Nicole dance and sing as though she had gone mad.

"Hey, come here. Check this out!" he whispered out to Ricky.

All this spinning around, singing and looking up to the sky had made Nicole feel quite dizzy so she stopped and took some deep breaths. When she felt she was alone, her eyes turned back upwards and she called out.

"Night, please come down. I want to see you!"

Ricky had now joined Andrew at the fence.

"Who, who is she talking to?" Andrew asked.

"I don't know," Ricky replied. "C'mon, let's go."

"Wait, wait!" Andrew said, looking a bit mischievous. "Let's make some noise or throw things. You know, just to scare her."

Ricky shook his head and grabbed his friend's arm to pull him away. He remarked, "She's not worth it."

"Okay, okay," Andrew grumbled.

When the boys had gone, Nicole was still looking up into the sky.

It happened again the next night, around the same time that Nicole stood out in the yard. Perhaps it was because she had practiced some and was more confident in her calling on Night that it didn't look as awkward as before. Ricky was there as well. This time he was alone as he watched Nicole from behind the fence. "I wonder what's up with that girl?" he asked himself.

After she had finished singing, she spoke up once more. "Where are you? I'm Nicole. You came down for my daddy. You can come down for me, can't you?...Night, I believe in you. Please come down and tell those people that my daddy is okay and he didn't make up Night."

Night remained silent.

)))) ● (((((

"Do you think Night likes me?" Nicole asked as she knelt on one of the chairs that had been placed at the edge of the front room. She was looking in a large mirror as she diplayed different facial expressions and poses. Auntie Ruth was watching television a few feet away.

"I beg your pardon?" her aunt asked.

"I don't think Night likes me."

Auntie Ruth got up and walked behind Nicole. She asked, "Now, why would you say that, Nicole?"

"I don't know. Sometimes, I think if I was older or looked prettier ---

Auntie Ruth interrupted Nicole. "Nicole, does it say anywhere in your father's journal that Night is concerned with appearances?"

"Um, no..."

"Well okay then. If it did matter, you look just fine, alright?"

Nicole nodded. "I recall your father saying he did a dance. Did you dance, Nicole?"

"Uh huh."

"And did you sing?"

"Oh yes. I tried to sing the song just the way I remembered Daddy singing it to me."

"Good, good," Auntie Ruth replied.

"Then what else do I gotta do?" Nicole asked.

Before trying to call on Night again the next night in the way she had done before, Nicole started to think. Maybe she was doing things right but maybe it wasn't in the right place. Night was in fact bigger than she knew. So once Auntie Ruth had turned into her room for the night, Nicole snuck out to find a better place to call on Night. She thought it would be alright since she was only planning to be gone for only a short time and not journey too far.

Nicole started out in one place and then to another one. She called on Night along the way. Farther and farther she searched for just the right spot. Since things often appear different in the night time, she was beginning to think she was lost. Just when Nicole was wondering if it was this house she passed, or another, it began to rain. And it RAINED!

"Oh no!" cried Nicole as the rain poured down over her.

Her feet were getting soaked, starting from the tiny hole on the top corner of her worn-out tennis shoes. After she had wiped the rain from her glasses, she saw a light coming from a diner across the street and down another block. Nicole pulled her jacket over her head and hurried towards that direction.

The rain continued.

Meanwhile, laughter and conversation filled this diner.
The customers, who acted as if they were old friends,
barely took notice of the table where Nicole sat. Although
her clothes looked almost dry and there was a steaming
cup of tea in front of her, Nicole lay her head on the table.
There was some water on her face. It was hard to tell,
unless thoroughly examined, if it was from the rain or from
tears.

Nicole didn't notice when the diner turned almost silent.
That's when she heard a voice speaking to her. It was a
lady's voice that was very pleasant... but not too sweet.

"Excuse me little girl. It's getting late. Shouldn't you be
home by now?"

Nicole still had her head on the table as she answered. "I
--- I'm waiting for someone."

"And who might that be?" the voice asked.

"I'm not sure," Nicole responded. "I went looking for her
and then it started raining so I came in here. I'll be on my
way home once it stops raining ma'am."

"Nicole, why did you call me down?"

Nicole gasped as she raised her head. Sitting across from
her at the table was Alison. Now it was difficult for Nicole
to describe how Alison looked like at that precise moment.
She was wearing a light blue dress and she was beautiful,
of course, but it was a kind of beauty that felt like it could

only be found in a dream. A lovely dream that by chance drifted out of place. This is why the others in the diner were speechless as they watched her.

"I feel it's necessary for me to ask that. I can't come down just for any reason," Alison spoke again.

A look of wonderment came upon Nicole's face.

"Pardon me. I'm Alison."

"Night?" Nicole said in a loud whisper as she leaned across the table.

Alison's smile was followed by a gracious nod. After gawking at her for a moment, Nicole reached out to touch Alison's arm. But before she did, Alison politely said, "Don't worry. I had to come down and be like one of you for you to truly believe."

Nicole wanted to speak some more but she had become aware of the others as they sat transfixed on Alison as well. That's when Nicole spoke in a softer voice, "Uhm, ma'am..."

"Please call me Alison."

"Alison. I --- I don't mean to be impolite, but it's important. I want to be sure."

"If I'm really Night?" Alison responded.

Nicole nodded while the others in the diner leaned closer towards the table where Nicole and Alison sat.

"Nicole, I believe it stopped raining."

After a good rain, it can still feel like it's raining for sometime later. However, there was a certain warmness that Nicole felt as she walked with Alison, that things were alright at that time. *This must have been how Daddy felt before*, she thought to herself. Being exactly nine-years-old, it may have been easier for Nicole to believe in the whole notion of Night than someone who is older and knows more. Even so, since this was the first time this kind of thing had happened to her, she did have lots of questions.

"Magic? Like some magic trick? What would you like me to do?" asked Alison

"I dunno. Maybe…"

"Night only does magic rarely just to show off. To tell you the truth, most of the magic people think Night does is the magic they make or what they believe."

"That's okay. I believe you're Night, Alison."

"Thank you Nicole. That's very kind of you."

Nicole smiled but it wasn't until they walked a bit farther that she spoke up again.

"It's just, just… Well, I wish more people would believe in Night than just me, Daddy and Auntie Ruth so that they won't laugh at us when we talk about it."

"Nicole, it's best that most people go on thinking Night is what it shows. Night wouldn't have it any other way. I'm taking a risk being with you now," Alison said in a more serious tone.

"I don't want you to get into any trouble."

After Nicole had said this, Alison gently placed her hand on the child's shoulder and said, "I like being here with you. I couldn't help it. It was like it was with your father calling on Night. I felt I had to come down. At the time he looked so sad and lonely, like you did before."

"I did?" Nicole responded.

"You mustn't feel alone when night comes, Nicole."

"Could you at least give me a sign to let me know you're near?"

"Well, I guess a little 'Show Off' magic every now and then would be alright." Alison returned with a wink.

It had been over ten blocks back to Auntie Ruth's house and another thirty steps up the sidewalk to her door. Alison was supporting Nicole as she opened the front gate.

"Nicole, you're home now."

"Already?" Nicole yawned.

As the two made their way towards the door, Alison spoke to Nicole, "I would imagine that your Auntie Ruth must be awfully worried."

"She was asleep when I left."

"Nicole!"

"Well? I had to find you!"

"Okay, I'll try not to make it so hard to find me next time. But you must make sure no one else is watching when you look for me."

In the front room of Auntie Ruth's house stood a grandfather clock. It was the most noticeable object when one first entered the house. Not so much because of the size of it or that it appeared to be a well-crafted clock, but because it made an unusually loud ticking sound. Nicole and Alison found this feature rather useful as they snuck through the house, up two flights of stairs and down the hall to Nicole's room.

"Auntie Ruth says I can decorate the room anyway I want to, but I'm still thinking," Nicole remarked.

Alison walked over to one of Nicole's paintings of night.

"Did you paint this, Nicole?"

"Yes. So, do you like it?"

"It's very nice," Alison replied. "But I think it's missing a few things."

Nicole picked up her painting to examine it a little closer. She turned the picture to different angles. Alison had walked to the window. She spoke to Nicole.

"You need to put in stars. A lot of stars. Otherwise, the sky would look empty."

Nicole set her painting down and had a seat on her bed.

"Do you know how many stars there are?" she asked Alison.

Alison answered, "I've tried counting all of them before but there are much too many, and there are other things I have to do."

"I wish I was Night. I'd go to so many far away places..." Nicole said.

"But then you'd never see the sun. Feel the sun. Never," Alison was quick to respond.

"It would be nice to be Night for a while, at least. I'd like to see the Realm of Night."

Alison smiled and she took a seat by Nicole on the bed.

"Daddy wrote that he's been to the Realm of Night. Did

you take him there?"

"I told your father as much as I could about the Realm of Night. Later he wrote some beautiful stories and songs about it. His heart was there, and I suppose that's almost as real as all of him."

Nicole fought to keep her eyes open as she laid her head down on her pillow.

"Could you tell me about the Realm of Night too?"

"Well, there are two parts of Night," Alison began. "Most people see only one because the parts appear to be the same. But there are two parts. There's the Other side of Night, that's where I'm from. Our purpose is to comfort the lonely, inspire the dreamer and to help bring those in love together."

As Alison continued her description, Nicole closed her eyes so she could get a better image of what Alison was telling her. And Alison had such a comforting voice. And when she spoke, Nicole pictured a fancy ballroom with beautiful women in elegant gowns and gentlemen in fancy suits. They danced and looked out the Windows in the Sky. *What a delight!* Nicole thought.

))) ● ((((

The next morning found Nicole safely tucked in her bed, although she was still wearing the clothes she had been wearing the night before. She woke with a start, as if someone had pinched her cheek, softly but firmly enough to awake her. Upon opening her eyes, she realized that it was just the sun coming through her window.

"Alison?" Nicole said as she sat up.

Nicole quickly grabbed her glasses from a night stand, got out of bed and looked around the room. "Alison, are you here?"

She moved out to the hallway and down the stairs where she noticed the door to Auntie Ruth's studio was open. "Auntie Ruth?" Nicole called out.

From within the room, Auntie Ruth responded, "I'm here, Nicole."

Nicole entered the studio and saw Auntie Ruth. Only Auntie Ruth. She had been working on a sculpture.

"Auntie Ruth, did you see where she went?" Nicole asked as she caught her breath.

"Did you lose someone?" Auntie Ruth asked as she continued sculpting.

"She was here."

"Who?"

"Alison," Nicole said as she stepped inside the studio.

Auntie Ruth turned around and stood up, and with the most emotion Nicole had seen in her, she asked, "Where? Where?"

"She came down for me yesterday!"

When Auntie Ruth looked at Nicole, she noticed that she appeared to not have changed her clothes from the evening when she last saw her. Perhaps the poor child was feeling ill, so Auntie Ruth wiped her hand on her apron and placed it on Nicole's forehead.

"Nicole, did you get enough sleep last night?"

"I saw her, Auntie Ruth. I know I did! 'Cept she didn't leave anything behind."

"I didn't think she would," Auntie Ruth remarked. "That is with her being Night and it being day right now."

"She promised that she'd come back. How long will it be 'til it's night?"

"Not for awhile," Auntie Ruth replied.

Nicole sighed. Auntie Ruth smiled as she left to wash her hands at the sink that was in her studio. She said to Nicole, "You really like her."

"She's wonderful."

"Did she look the way your father described her in his journal?"

"Yes, but she's prettier! Much prettier than what Daddy wrote."

"Well, we'll see about that. But for now, why don't you go back up, change into some new clothes and we'll meet for breakfast."

Nicole turned and headed for the door. Before she left, she said to her aunt, "You'll see, Auntie Ruth."

It was 7:30, more than one hour after Nicole had called on Night. She thought Alison certainly would come now that they had been acquainted. Now that they were friends. Well, Nicole believed them to be friends. But when Alison didn't show up, she couldn't help but feel some disappointment.

Alison said she had a lot of things to do. Yeah, I'm sure that's it. Nicole reasoned to herself. *She'll be here.*

Nicole went inside a while later with no luck after she called Night and watched a whole episode of Auntie Ruth's favorite show. And then she read the first part of a book and tried to find other things to do while she waited. Now it was two and a half hours later, and Alison still hadn't shown.

The first time something happens, it sometimes doesn't feel real. Especially if that something was as fantastic as her meeting with Alison. So sometimes it takes a second time to happen just to make sure. Nicole tried to remember all that happened last night, from the diner to the streets to ---

"Nicole, I think that maybe it's good for you to go to bed now," Auntie Ruth said as she placed her hand on Nicole's arm.

"But Auntie Ruth..." Nicole started. But when Nicole saw Auntie Ruth's face, she felt that it wasn't the time to argue since her Aunt had been kind to her since she arrived. Nicole arose in a melancholy manner and headed toward the stairs.

"It's night upstairs too you know," Auntie Ruth called out to her.

Nicole laid in bed dressed in her nightgown, staring at the ceiling. No happy thoughts would come to her mind. She had just closed her eyes for a moment when she heard a tap on her window. Nicole's curiosity was bigger than her fear, making her forget that she was on the third floor. When Nicole had gotten to the window, she saw a swarm of fireflies flying in concentric circles until at once, they formed a heart.

"Alison!" Nicole exclaimed.

Nicole raced down the stairs, turning on the lights as she went down.

"Auntie Ruth! She's here!" Nicole shouted out.

The first thing Nicole did was open the front door. When she saw that Alison wasn't there, she ran to the back door. And when she opened that door, she found Alison waiting for her just outside. Nicole rushed over to greet her.

"Alison, I found you!"

"I told you that I'd try to come down when I could," Alison responded.

"There's so much more I have to ask you, like…"

*Creek…*The sound of the back door opening, interrupted Nicole. They turned to see Auntie Ruth. She wore a purple robe and curlers as she sheepishly peeked out from behind the door.

"That's my Auntie Ruth," Nicole said. "It's okay, Alison. She believes in Night too."

Alison moved closer to where Auntie Ruth stood and

with a warm smile, she said "Hello Ruth."

"You were right, Nicole. She is real," Auntie Ruth said, trying to hold back her astonishment. "I'm sorry, where are my manners? How should I address you? Your Nightness? Madame Night…"

"If you would like, you can call me Alison."

There's a poem that Lord Byron wrote a long time ago. The first part goes:

> *She walks in beauty, like the night.*
> *Of cloudless climes and starry skies;*
> *And all that's best of dark and bright*
> *Meet in her aspect and her eyes:*
> *Thus mellowed to the tender light*
> *Which heaven to guady day denies.*

Perhaps this poem helped inspire Nicole's father when he was writing *A Little Bit About Night*. Whatever it was, it wasn't hard to see that by just looking at Alison moving down here, she could inspire hundreds of words. She was a vision to behold.

In order to keep a scene such as the one in the diner from occurring again, Nicole and Alison tried to stay in the shadows when they roamed about. And if avoiding being in the light proved difficult, they would move away from the place as swiftly as possible.

This prevented others from seeing Alison for the most part but there were those fortunate few who were able to catch more than a glimpse of her. One such person was the 14-year-old boy who lived next door to Auntie Ruth.

The wind that afternoon blew trash can lids and old scraps of paper and might have even blown Nicole away too had she been any smaller. She was able to make her way up the sidewalk to Auntie Ruth's house and had arrived at the front gate when a voice from behind called out to her.

"Hey!"

When Nicole turned around, she realized it was Ricky. He brought his bike to a screeching halt a few feet away.

"Hi Nicole, isn't it?" Ricky said to her.

"That's me."

"I'm Ricky. Ricky from next door."

"I know."

"Hey, about the other day, when you passed by ---"

"Yeah," Nicole said with a pout.

"I was thinking, maybe we got off on the wrong foot."

"I thought you were very rude."

"Well, you know how things are," Ricky tried to explain.

"Yes, I do," Nicole said before turning toward the front gate. But before she could reach the latch, Ricky spoke up again.

"Wait, I'm sorry. Listen, I was wondering if we could

talk?"

"About what?" Nicole sighed.

"About what? There's this lady I've been seeing coming to your house the last couple of nights."

"What do you know about her?!" Nicole said sharply, speaking over the wind.

"Whoa, it's cool. I just wanted to know if she's a cousin or something."

"Maybe."

"I think she's totally hot. She's ---" Ricky said with a grin.

"Well, she's too old for you. And, she's way too sophisticated for you." Nicole remarked.

"Yeah, right now she is. But, you know, it could happen."

Nicole gave Ricky the once over before rolling her eyes.

"Hey, I'm really not that bad. I could be charming too," Ricky said. He then began to sing a love song. Nicole raised her hand to him.

"What do you want?" she asked.

"Nicole, I was hoping that maybe you could introduce us."

"What? To you and your friends?"

"Them? I don't even like them," Ricky answered. "I just hang around them and all. They don't even know about her. No, it'll just be me."

"I don't know," Nicole responded.

"You see, there're no women around here like her or at school. I haven't seen many anyway. I've never hung out or been friends with someone that beautiful. I'd like to know how it feels."

Nicole looked up at the sky.

"So how about it?" Ricky asked."

Right then, Nicole wanted to say "No, I won't share Alison. She's my Night not yours!" But she didn't. Maybe Night was meant to come down for Ricky. She couldn't say. Nicole looked at him. He didn't appear to be the rude boy like before. Nicole opened her mouth but before she could speak, Auntie Ruth's voice could be heard calling from the house.

"Nicole, could you come here? I need to tell you something. Oh, hello Ricky. And how are you today?"

"Who really knows?" Ricky said as he lifted up his hands.

Nicole opened the gate and entered the house. Once inside, Auntie Ruth closed the door and spoke. "The hospital where your father's at told me that he's getting better."

"Will I get to see him?" Nicole asked with some excitement.

"Soon, but they said that we shouldn't bring up the topic of Night."

))) ● ● (((

When Nicole came to stay at her aunt's house, Auntie Ruth had promised to take her to a park. It took almost two weeks but she kept her promise to Nicole. It was a few days later that Nicole would return to that park with Alison. Now Nicole may not have seen as many parks as some, but she had seen enough parks to know which were good ones and which were not.

"Fat ducks are good for eating but it's not good for park ducks to be fat. Auntie Ruth said that I shouldn't feed the ducks here too much, even the babies," Nicole said.

It was night and the park was empty and quiet. Alison had asked Nicole to describe how the park looked like the day she went there. "Over there is where I met Polly and Karen. They asked me if I wanted to be their friend and I said okay."

"That's nice," Alison smiled.

"Polly's brother George and some other boys were playing on the swings. They were showing off, trying to see who could swing the highest. They didn't let anyone else swing when they were there."

Alison nodded and had a look around, trying to picture what Nicole was saying.

"There were people running, and people riding bikes and skating. Let's see. And there were moms pushing their babies in strollers," Nicole continued. "Auntie Ruth took some pictures. Do you want to see them?"

"I've seen a few pictures taken when it was daytime that your father showed me. I guess I'm not as good at imagining things like him. I need more than a picture to know what something is like."

"Hmmmm," is all Nicole could think of saying then. She

was so happy just being with Alison that she had forgotten that she and Alison were not the same and they would never truly be the same as long as Alison was Night.

They walked down the pathway and Alison talked about places she was able to go with Nicole's father. Nicole thought, if Alison was able to come down, she should be able to see the day, shouldn't she?

The two had gone back to the part of the park where the playground was nearby. Nicole ran to the swing set. She called out to Alison as she did.

"C'mon Alison."

Nicole sat down and began to swing. In a moment, Alison was there beside her. With a smile, Nicole motioned Alison to sit on the next swing over, which she did. When she noticed that Alison wasn't moving the swing, Nicole instructed.

"First you have to push off with your feet. And then you go forward and back. Forward and back."

This might have been the first time Alison had ever been on a swing but she seemed like a natural.

"You're doing good Alison!" Nicole laughed.

They swung for a few moments, moving faster and faster but not too high. After a while, the swinging slowed down and then finally to a stop.

"That was fun, Nicole. Thank you," Alison said.

Nicole nodded, and while catching her breath, she said, "Alison, I'll try to figure out a way for you to see the day."

"Okay Nicole, that will be nice," Alison said, smiling the way people do when they're trying to believe in something that seems impossible.

Alison got up with Nicole following after. The two had just gotten back on the pathway when they noticed a small light coming towards them. It looked a bit shaky when they first had seen it but it was getting closer and the distant patter of feet began sounding like echoing stomps. Soon it became clear that it was a policeman, and when he had a better look at Nicole and Alison he shouted.

"You shouldn't be here!"

Nicole turned to run but Alison calmly grabbed her hand, and like a magician who has spent years and years practicing her craft, Alison waved her hand in front of them. The policeman stopped in his tracks because they have become invisible to him.

"Where'd they go? Hello, hello...?" the policeman spoke.

He examined the area, looking for clues from the vanishing duo. Alison led Nicole past the policeman. Before they made their departure, Nicole turned around and waved at him.

"Well I'll be," the policeman remarked as he stood there and scratched his head.

Most of the thoughts Nicole had at breakfast the next morning were about what she had told Alison the night before, specifically how she was going to help Alison see the day. If there was a way, it was obvious that her father hadn't found it or else Alison would be down here with them maybe having breakfast. But maybe he wrote something that might give her a clue that could lead to another clue that would lead to a way. So after she had cleaned her plate, Nicole had found her father's journal *A Little Bit About Night* which she had hidden beneath her suitcase and some boxes in her closet. This is the passage, which had the words *Almost Dawn* written on top of the page. She read:

Alison wants to see the sun. That's what she tells me when I see her. Alison wants to see the sun, even though she's Night. I told Alison that if she sees the sun she might die. It's my fault because I told her how wonderful the sun is.

Alison doesn't know anything about death and thinks she won't be Night if she sees the sun. I believe what Alison says. I don't care if it sounds silly. She makes me believe. So I told her that I would hold her hand when the sun came up.

We tried, but Alison couldn't make it. It was too hard for her. But we'll try again another time, because Alison wants to see the sun.

Dark and the Other

Alison didn't come every time Nicole called on Night. This was a realization that Nicole had learned to live with. Any disappointment of Alison not showing up was notably lessened because of two reasons. First, Nicole now knew Alison was real, and second, Alison was the most amazing person she had ever met, and most likely would meet. So when Alison did not appear that night, Nicole thought she'd wait just a little while longer before going inside.

But there was something about that night that made Nicole feel it was not like the others. The clouds covered almost all the stars, which of course was not unusual. But these clouds seemed in a way... darker. Nicole let her imagination run wild, making her think that the clouds formed bony fingers and scary faces. The wind blowing through the trees sounded like moaning, almost whispering, *Nicole...*

"Alison?" Nicole murmured. But Alison was not to be seen. How Nicole wished that Alison would come to comfort her at that moment. Nicole couldn't wait any longer. That's when she heard ---

"Nicole, Night can be a very dangerous place," a dark, menacing voice spoke from somewhere around her.

"Who's there?" Nicole asked meekly. She scanned the shadows and the light, and when she turned towards the house she saw him.

"The trouble with inviting Night down is you just never know who might come. Well, look here. It's me," the man arrogantly said as he came out from the darkness of the shadows. He reminded Nicole of Alison but at the same time, he was altogether different. He was beautiful like she was but he appeared more like a nightmare than a dream. His piercing eyes glared at her.

"Wh---who are you?" Nicole asked as she tried not to look at him.

"No, no, no. You don't need to know that now," he said wagging his finger at her.

"Where's Alison? Is she…"

"Where's Alison? Where's Alison?" the man said in a high, mocking voice. "You speak as though you own her. Like she belongs down here with you. Would you imagine that? One of you, owning Night."

"She's my friend," Nicole explained.

Nicole didn't know at the time but this man speaking to her was named David, and he was from the Dark side of Night. And when David smiled at her, she knew she would not like him.

"I don't like you at all. Go away!" Nicole demanded.

"Why, I just got here. Oh no, not yet." David laughed.

"Go away!" Nicole spoke louder.

"I heard you the first time. Let's see what else we can do."

Ricky, the boy who lived next door, just so happened to be outside when he heard the commotion coming from Auntie Ruth's backyard. He moved over to the fence and peered over the top to see David on one knee as he had a hold of Nicole's hand.

"Let me go!" Nicole cried.

"I just want to be liked. Won't you be my friend? You're Alison's friend, aren't you? And we're both Night. Oh please, please, please. Have a heart," David said with innocent eyes.

"Well…" Nicole began. But when she looked down at her hand in David's it appeared that there were spiders coming out of his hands onto hers. Nicole screamed and pulled her hand away from his. She turned the other direction, making David laugh some more. He swiftly moved in front of her and showed her his clean hand.

"See it's fake. It wasn't real. Fooled you. Made you look."

"Leave me alone. I want to see Alison."

"Oh that again. Well let me tell you something Missy, Alison doesn't like you now. Never did, nope. And… would you excuse me?"

At the fence, Ricky was almost over the top as he tried to see what was going on.

"Nicole?" Ricky called out.

In a flash, David was a few feet away from him. He put on a face of a man that looked like he'd been drowned for several days. When David opened his eyes he said,

"You got a problem? Get outta here!"

"Ahhhh!" Ricky shouted as he fell off the fence and scrambled to the light of his house.

"Run boy, run. I'm right behind you!" David hissed after him.

Once David turned around, Nicole could see that he was back to how he looked before. She was a few steps closer to the back door when David asked her.

"Where are you going Nicole?"

"That wasn't very nice." Nicole remarked.

"That? That was nothing, You can't imagine what I have planned for you, Nicole," David spoke and this time he looked serious. He seemed to glide across the backyard towards her.

"Auntie Ruth." Nicole spoke up.

"Looks like it's just you and me kid," David continued.

"Auntie Ruth!" Nicole said louder still.

"I wonder how long it is until morning..." David remarked. He was close enough to where he could reach out and touch her. And then his eyes widened.

"AUNTIE RUTH!" Nicole screamed out.

At that, the porch light came on. Auntie Ruth stepped out and raced over to Nicole.

"What, what is it Nicole? What's going on?" Auntie Ruth said with a look of concern.

Nicole cautiously looked around. David was no longer with them. Auntie Ruth put her arm around Nicole who had her arms crossed and was shaking. As Auntie Ruth led her inside the house she asked.

"Are you okay, Nicole? You scared me half to death!"

There was nothing out of the ordinary about the morning. There were still a few clouds in the sky along with a slight breeze but for Nicole, it felt like the brightest and most welcoming morning she had ever known.

She had reached the last flight of stairs when she heard a man's voice. It was a voice she had not heard before and it was very early. He was talking to Auntie Ruth.

"Now I don't want to worry you here, but there may be a prowler," The man said.

"A prowler? My goodness!" Auntie Ruth gasped.

Once Nicole had entered the room where the conversation was taking place, she noticed it was a police officer speaking with Auntie Ruth.

"The report says, somebody saw a strange man being not so friendly with your niece. I'm here to check it out," The police officer said.

"Would you hold on a sec, I'll call her,"

As Auntie Ruth turned around she saw Nicole standing at the far end of the room.

"Nicole will you come here please?" Auntie Ruth asked. "This is Officer…

"Hankins," the police officer remarked.

Nicole stopped and stood beside Auntie Ruth.

"Hi ya, Nicole. I'm Officer Hankins. I have a few questions here I was hoping you can help me with, okay?"

There wasn't a noticeable response from Nicole as she moved closer to Auntie Ruth. Officer Hankins cleared his throat and continued.

"Nicole can you tell me if you've seen anyone or anything strange around here?"

"What do you mean?" Nicole asked, staring straight ahead.

"There may have been a prowler," Officer Hankins spoke in a lower tone.

"I didn't see a prowler," Nicole responded.

"You sure? You don't have to be scared now."

"Yes sir," Nicole nodded.

Officer Hankins rubbed his chin as he looked at Nicole. He bent down towards the girl and then cocked his head at a slight angle to the left so that his ear came closer to Nicole just in case she would have anything more to say. After a brief moment of hearing nothing, the officer straightened up and looked over to Auntie Ruth.

"Even so, I --- I'd feel better if I had a look around to see if there are any signs of forced entry and to show you any place where he might enter."

"Well sure," said Auntie Ruth as she followed Officer Hankins to another part of the room. Nicole remained where she was standing.

That night would be unlike those prior. All the lights were on as Nicole thoroughly checked the room. She used a long stick that she found to poke around the closet to make sure it was just her clothes and shoes there. Then it was behind the desk and curtains.

With her eyes closed, Nicole knelt beside her bed and

clasped her hands. She opened them slowly to grab a water gun on a chair and squirted underneath her bed to make sure anything or anyone hiding down there would feel uncomfortable and choose to leave.

Nicole left the lamp on and once she felt safe enough to lie in her bed, she pulled the covers over her face. This is how she welcomed night for some time to come.

))) ● ((((

One of the biggest gatherings of the summer happened to be at Auntie Ruth's church. The planning committee was very proud of how things turned out. They were able to bring in a fairly popular band from the city to play at this year's event. The smell of roasted corn, funnel cakes and other food tempted the senses. It was estimated that close to one thousand people were there that night.

This also was the first time in seventeen days that Nicole had been out at night since her unfortunate encounter with David. But tonight she didn't look the same as before. Instead of the odd-looking, lonely girl, she appeared laughing, running around with her friends (which is common for nine-year-old girls). In fact, if one would see Nicole that night underneath all the lights of the bazaar, he or she would think she was some typical girl, one of the crowd. Perhaps Nicole had even outgrown Night. It was like a favorite toy or an imaginary friend she had let go of and was now a happy memory.

"I'll be right over there Auntie Ruth," Nicole said while pointing at a building that looked dark as compared to the others at the bazaar.

"Okay. But don't stay too long. We'll be leaving here soon,"Auntie Ruth responded.

Nicole promised as she headed by herself towards the building. It was later in the night and the bazaar appeared to be winding down. However, there were still enough people around to make Nicole feel secure.

The building looked to be a small storage area, not much bigger than a two car garage. It was not attractive to look at but it was functional. Nicole waited for a couple to leave before she snuck around the corner. The sounds of the bazaar could still be heard but Nicole took one more peek around the corner to make certain. She knew she had to hurry if she was going to do what she had planned.

"Here it goes," Nicole said as she anxiously looked up into the sky and said,"Night, please come down."

Nicole remained standing where she was but she clenched her fists and closed her eyes, preparing for whatever would come. It may have been only a passing moment when she heard,

"Hello Nicole."

When Nicole opened her eyes, she looked towards the direction where someone looking like Alison stood.

"Alison, is that you?" Nicole asked.

Alison answered."Who did you think it was?"

"I was afraid," Nicole said.

"I know. That was a mean trick David played on you. He wouldn't tell me all he did, but he said, 'Don't expect her to be calling on Night again'. So I watched and waited.'"

"David, is that his name?"

"The one and only," Alison responded.

"Are you like him?"

"Nicole, do you remember when I told you about the two parts of Night?"

Nicole thought about it before she answered. "Uh, yeah."

"Well, David is from the Dark side and I'm from the Other side," Alison explained.

"So he's from the bad side and you're from the good side?"

"Not necessarily," Alison replied. "Some of my friends are from the Dark. That's just who they are. They don't always mean to scare people. They just happen to be there when people are afraid."

"But David will come back when you're not around. I know it," Nicole said with a worried look on her face.

Alison took a step closer to Nicole as she spoke. "He'll never come down here unless he feels he absolutely has to. David hates coming down. He said this form is heavy and rather uncomfortable. He doesn't have the freedom to move about the way he thinks the Dark should."

"How about you?"

"I don't mind," Alison answered. "Sometimes I get very tired down here, but I don't mind."

"So David will never come back?" Nicole asked.

"I can't promise that Nicole. But if he does, just look him in the eyes and say, 'Alison told me that I don't need to be afraid of you, and I'm not?'"

"Will that work?"

"Let's just say, there are some parts of the Dark that are so arrogant that if they know that you're not afraid of them, they'll pretend that they don't know who you are and go away."

"I just say, 'Alison said I don't need to be afraid of you and I'm not?'"

"Do you think you can do that?"

Nicole smiled and nodded her head as she ran to embrace Alison. The sounds from the bazaar made them aware that it wasn't quite over. Alison spoke up.

"Looks like they're having quite a celebration over there."

"It's so much fun," Nicole took a step towards the bazaar.

"It looks very enjoyable."

"Come with me, Alison. There's this ride you've got to try."

"Nicole, I can't. Not just yet."

"But you said that you wanted to feel what day is like. This isn't daytime, but right now it's almost like it," Nicole said as she grabbed Alison's hand.

The names of two of Nicole's friends she was with at the bazaar were Polly and Karen. When they noticed that Nicole was no longer with them and not around Auntie Ruth, they went searching for her. In a short time, they found the small building where Nicole was. It appeared that she was not by herself at the time.

"There you are Nicole," Polly called out.

By the time they had reached her, Nicole was alone. Karen asked, "Who were you talking to?"

"That's weird. Karen, did you see?" Polly asked with a confused look.

Nicole spoke up as she walked back to the bazaar. "C'mon, let's go back."

))) 🌓 ● 🌗 (((

Never once in his fourteen years has anyone ever scared Ricky the way David had that one night."It had to be because it happened so fast and it was dark," Ricky tried to assure himelf. No one would believe him when he told them what he saw. Not his father, not the officer. He would show them alright. Whoever that was who scared him had to come back, so almost every night, Ricky kept watch of any out of the ordinary going ons at Auntie Ruth's house.

"Well, I'm glad that's cleared up," Auntie Ruth said as she finished mending a hole on Nicole's sweater.

"Me too. Now I get to see more of Alison," Nicole smiled.

"And now you don't have to worry about seeing the Dark again. But I guess it wouldn't be Night without the Dark, would it?" Auntie Ruth said as she handed Nicole her sweater.

As Nicole was putting on her sweater, Auntie Ruth asked,"By the way, where is Alison?"

"She told me that she'd wait outside. It gets too bright for her in here sometimes," Nicole answered.

The light from the street lamp barely reached Auntie Ruth's garden. Here was where Alison stood at the time. In shadows, things don't always apear quite clear, but Ricky knew that it wasn't Auntie Ruth nor Nicole that he saw in the garden then. His heart raced faster with each beat when he snuck up on Night and threw a blanket over her.

"I got him!" Ricky exclaimed, hardly knowing what had happened.

Nicole had just stepped out of the front door when she saw the struggle that was going on.

"Ricky, what are you doing?!" Nicole cried.

"I caught the prowler! Call the police!"

"What?"

"Don't tell me that you don't know what I'm talking about! You saw him just as plain as I did," Ricky remarked while trying to hold down the blanket.

"Let her go!" Nicole said in a voice with both anger and concern.

"You see, I knew he'd back. And when I saw him lurking around here, I was ready for him this time Nicole. I was ready," Ricky said proudly.

"Let her go!" pleaded Nicole as she gave Ricky a push.

"Not so tough now, are you?" Ricky snarled.

Using all her weight, Nicole was finally able to get Ricky

off Alison. She removed the blanket.

"Wait! What are you doing? Call the..."

Something absolutely phenomenal happened when Alison emerged from underneath the blanket. Nicole and Ricky noticed that she had partially faded! Alison clenched her fist and appeared solid once more. Ricky fell to the ground and sat astonished.

"Wha --- what's going on here?" Ricky stammered.

"Ricky, this is Alison," Nicole spoke.

Rising, Alison walked towards Ricky. She appeared to glow more brightly than normal. It appeared as if she was regaining her strength.

Ricky covered his head and cried, "I'm sorry. Oh God, am I sorry. Don't kill me, please!"

With a gracious appearance, Alison offered Ricky her hand. "It's okay Ricky, you can get up now."

"Oh, it's you," Ricky said once he had gotten a closer look at Alison. "I couldn't tell from back there."

"Ricky, how much do you know about Night?" Alison asked.

)))) ● ((((

There is a last page of the journal, *A Little Bit About Night*, that Nicole's father wrote. But it most likely wasn't the end. For one, there were still a few more blank pages left and there is no where on the last page that said something like --- "The End." or "This is the FINAL PAGE---" This leaves one to believe that Nicole's father had not finished it. Since the journal didn't contain a large number of written pages, Nicole was able to read it several times. What came to her attention is that her father never once mentioned anything about David or the Dark side of Night. Why hadn't Alison told Nicole's father about the two parts of Night like she told her and now Ricky? If Alison did reveal this fact, had Nicole's father forgotten it like Nicole had?

Nicole read the last page of her father's journal before she went to bed that night:

There are secrets that Alison hasn't told me. She says she can't tell me everything or else she would get in trouble. I forgive her. She is Night by the way. Alison says she would tell me what she could, when the time is right. This will have to do until I can find a way for us to be together for more than just the night.

I try not to wonder about these secrets. It's sometimes hard but Alison makes me feel like it will be okay if I just wait. I think I'm in love with Alison. That's my secret.

Grownups

"Nicole, I hope you're not getting a hard time when people ask you where your father is when in fact, I'm here in this, this nut house. I wouldn't blame you if you thought I was crazy. You're old enough to know what's real," Nicole's father said, speaking on a telephone. The room he was sitting in was painted in a color that could wipe away the cheer from most anybody.

"I tell them that you're doing research on some top secret things," Nicole said with a smile on a phone on the other end.

"I like it. Good thinking, Nicole," her father said with a laugh.

Before getting any further into Night, now might be a good time to discuss the time when Nicole's father first met Alison and about the circumstances that brought him into this nut house. This given the fact that he is the reason *this* story of Night came about in the first place.

Nicole's father's name is Marc Alexander. He, like Nicole, wasn't one to stand out from the crowd. He was handsome, but not extremely handsome so he wouldn't normally be the one chosen for the lead in the school play nor the one picked first to play basketball. But by finding more about who he is, one could tell why his wife fell in love with him and why Alison came down several times to meet him. Marc has a boyish charm about him and wit but probably most of all it was because he is kind.

It had been four months and five days since Marc's wife Sarah, Nicole's mother, had passed away. That's when he thought about calling on Night. His heart was broken in a way that even if the pieces were eventually put back together, they wouldn't fit quite right. Marc recalled hearing about Night from a man that he had done work for. Now almost everybody would dismiss the whole notion of Night as a childish tale, but when Marc looked into this man's eyes, it was hard for him not to believe. To keep his mind off his wife's death, Marc thought about what this man had told him and called upon Night. That's when Alison visited him.

"Am I correct to say that you are Night?" Marc asked the first time she visited.

"Yes, I'm Night. Alison, if you want to be specific about the whole thing," Alison answered.

Needless to say, Marc was enchanted when his eyes first were set upon Alison but it was her voice that he would remember most. It sounded like a song to him. A sweet, light song. It lifted him up like a spell was cast on him. This was certainly not Alison's intention. She came down to visit Marc to aid in healing his heart so that he can move on like she had done for several others in the past. But when he sang for her and told the wonderful things about the day and the sun, Alison became unaware how many times she had visited Marc. For Night, this was a precarious thing. Alison had gone down far more than her purpose, causing rumors to be spread of Alison no longer wishing to be Night so she could see the sun.

To put an end to this kind of talk swiftly, David of

the Dark was sent to pay Marc a visit (as was the case when one would wander too far into Night). When Marc called on Night, as was his usual custom, it was David who came down that time. Everything appeared as it was before because he had disguised himself as Alison. Marc never knew until it was too late. David lied and tricked Marc slowly, and deeply, making him think he was seeing and hearing things. While he was doing this, David's appearance changed from the beautiful, sweet Alison to the most hideous witch Marc's fear could ever conjure.

"That's it. He has gone mad! He's a loon!" his friends and others had concluded when they found Marc the next morning, muttering nonsense about Night. "The toll from his wife's death was too much for him to bear."

It was determined, and Marc would be forced to agree with, that he would be leaving his daughter Nicole for time deemed necessary to recover in one of the best mental hospitals around. Hubert Charles, Esquire was put in charge of finding a suitable place for Nicole to stay during this period. It was a blessing that Marc's only living relative at the time was located. Her name is Ruth Dowling. She is Marc's half sister and who is a number of years older than him.

This is how Nicole and Marc got to where they were at this time and why they could only talk over the phone.

"I don't think you're crazy, Daddy," Nicole said.

"Super! Hey Nicole how would you feel if after I get out of here, we go to Vancouver?" Marc asked.

"Where's that?" Nicole returned.

"Vancouver. We've been there before, you know. Your mother, you and me. You were probably too young, but I tell you, it's beautiful."

"What would we do there?" Nicole wondered.

"Do there? Why, we'd live," Marc answered. "I have all these plans and I know people there."

"How about Night?"

"You know something, Nicole? I don't think about Night much anymore. Night stopped coming when I let go of those delusions, you know, crazy thoughts. At least that's what Judith says."

"Who Judith?" Nicole asked.

"Judith is one of the doctors who works here. She doesn't want me to call her anything besides 'Judith'. I think you two might like each other."

"You stopped believing in Night?!"

"I'm trying to. It's the only way I can get out of here. With Judith's help, it's getting easier."

"Daddy! Night came down for me. I met Alison, and Auntie Ruth saw her too!"

"Nicole, stop! We --- we'll talk about this later, okay?"

)))) ● ● ((((

If a person believes in something --- really, really believes in something, does this make that something real? And what if that someone who got her to believe in that something says that he no longer believes in it anymore... Does it make it less real or not real at all? These were the thoughts Nicole had as she was getting ready for bed. It had been a long day for her so she thought she would not call on Night this time. But it was hard not to think about Night.

"Daddy can't stop believing in Night," Nicole groaned.

She pinched herself twice when she first met Alison just to make sure she was awake at the time. She even had more proof when Auntie Ruth and then Ricky saw Alison. All three couldn't have been dreaming about the same thing at the same time, could they?

"Now if Daddy could only see Alison, he'll ----"

CRASH! There was a startling sound coming from Auntie Ruth's front yard.

Nicole hurried to the window to see what it was. She opened the curtains. It was dark but she could tell well enough what she saw. Out on the front lawn, Ricky was pushing Andrew behind a bush. There was also another, smaller boy with them. Ricky was whispering something to him and pointing to another bush.

"Ricky?!" Nicole cried out.

Down the stairs and through the front door Nicole went. She stopped just in front of the bush where Ricky and Andrew hid. It had not completely covered them.

"Ricky, come out from those bushes!" Nicole demanded.

There was no sound. Nicole spoke again.

"I know you're there. I can see your feet."

A few more seconds passed before Ricky stumbled from

behind the bush. After spitting a leaf from his mouth and dusting himself off, Ricky said, "Oh, hi Nicole."

"Ricky, what are you doing here?"

"Well, I was..." Ricky started, trying to hide his embarrassment.

"And who is he?" Nicole demanded, pointing at the other pair of shoes behind the bushes.

"Him?" Ricky questioned.

Andrew stood up and approached Nicole.

"Hey girlie. If, if you're seeing some kind of sighting, you can't keep it for yourself. You can't. It won't be ethical or whatever," said Andrew.

Nicole turned over to Ricky and said, "You told him?"

"Of course he told me," Andrew said as he put his arm around Ricky's shoulder. "We're best buds. We tell each other everything."

Nicole looked to the ground and shook her head. Ricky tried to speak to her in a calm voice but it was cracking.

"Okay, I tried not to tell anyone like you and Alison said, okay? But I couldn't stop thinking about Alison and Night. I had to tell someone, but I knew no one would believe me and well, now Andrew knows. You've gotta let him see Alison. Please!"

Andrew rubbed his hands together as he spoke to Nicole. "So when do we get to see her?"

"Night can't come down for just anyone." Nicole responded. "You have to ---"

Some rustling from another bush was heard and it

interrupted Nicole. Kevin, the younger boy with a crew cut emerged.

"Hey, how long do I have to stay hiding? It stinks. It smells like a cat did it back there," Kevin spoke.

"And who is he?" Nicole said, putting her hand to her forehead.

"That's my little bro, Kevin," Andrew answered.

"Ricky, you told him too?"

"I didn't tell him, alright?" Ricky tried to explain. "He was in the next room. He heard everything. He wouldn't shut up."

"I think it's cool," Kevin spoke up.

Ricky turned to Kevin and threatened, "Kevin, if you told anyone, I'm going to kill you."

Anyone who knew anything about Kevin knew that he could not keep a secret. Telling Kevin a secret would be like placing posters of what was said around town in large letters. That's why no one told Kevin any secrets. This made Kevin even more eager to find out about things. Ricky now remembered this when he heard footsteps along with the sound of children approaching Auntie Ruth's house.

"Is this the place?" a boy's voice spoke.

"I think so," answered a girl.

Ricky turned towards Kevin. "I'm going to kill you!"

While Andrew held Ricky back from killing his brother, Kevin spoke.

"Do you know what happens in this town? Nothing. I felt real important when I told people about this and they believed me. I guess word spread."

Even after Auntie Ruth had turned on the front light, it was difficult to count how many children showed up at her yard that night. All Nicole knew was that there were much too many. The chants of **NIGHT - NIGHT - NIGHT** filled the air while Ricky chased Kevin around the dark yard.

The commotion grew louder and louder, so much that Auntie Ruth had to shout, "Nicole, what's going on here?"

Nicole couldn't answer because soon she was surrounded by Polly and some of the other children. They were asking her questions, almost all at the same time.

"Nicole, why didn't you tell us that something this big is happening to you?"

"Yeah! Everybody's talking about it!"

"Can you really bring down these people from this Night place?"

Nicole SCREAMED.

There were cars that came that night. They were cars filled with grownups in them with angry looks on their faces when they found out what was happening. One by one, they took the children back into the cars and away from Auntie Ruth's yard. One of those grownups was Polly's mother. She wore a short, dark blue dress and far too much makeup that made her face almost shine in the dark. The shoes she had on that night made it difficult for her to walk on the grass as she made her way over to Polly.

"Mother," Polly uttered.

"What is the meaning of this, sneaking off in the middle

of the night?!" Polly's mother snapped.

"It's not even nine," Polly remarked.

"Hush! You made me miss my date," Polly's mother continued."What are you doing here anyway?"

"A miracle is going to happen," Karen spoke up. "Nicole is going to bring down Night!"

They all turned towards Nicole.

"You! You're the one who told them all this nonsense," Polly's mother spat in an unpleasant tone.

"It's not nonsense," Nicole spoke.

"You know very well that you made it up. The new girl in town, pleading for attention."

"I didn't make it up," Nicole said in a stronger voice.

"Come now!" Polly's mother said,"You mean to tell me that you actually believe in this, what does she call it?"

"Night," Karen said.

"Night," Polly's mother continued. "Why can't you tell the truth little girl and tell these children that there is no such thing as Night?"

"There is a Night and they came down to me but they will NEVER come down for mean people like you!" Nicole cried.

Polly's mother was not ready for the words that came out of Nicole's mouth and the audacity of how they were said. Her departure from Auntie Ruth's yard began with an upwards turn of her nose followed by a sharp turn. She grabbed Polly's arm and scolded her as they left.

The type of scene that had occurred was frowned upon

by those who live in Auntie Ruth's neighborhood so it was not a surprise to see the flashing lights of a police car show up. Once again it was Officer Hankins on the scene. After a wave hello to Auntie Ruth, he ushered the remaining children out with a megaphone.

"GO HOME KIDS. THERE IS NO PARTY HERE. GO HOME --- THAT MEANS YOU TOO."

Ricky walked over to Nicole hanging his head with slouched shoulders. He said softly to Nicole,"I'm sorry." He then looked up into the sky and said, "I'm sorry." Ricky's sorrow seemed short-lived when he spotted Kevin across the street. He was gone soon enough.

Auntie Ruth waved goodbye to Officer Hankins once the last of the children had left. The night was quiet for a little while before the phone from Auntie Ruth's house rang. She closed the gate and turned to Nicole.

"Are you going to be alright, Nicole?"

Nicole answered with a nod. Auntie Ruth put her hand on Nicole's shoulder but another phone ring distracted her.

"Okay, okay. I'm coming," Auntie Ruth responded as she headed towards the house. "Come in soon Nicole, okay?"

Since Nicole didn't feel quite like going inside just yet, she thought she might as well call on Night. She closed her eyes and counted to ten. "One, two..." Once she reached ten, she opened her eyes to make sure she was alone and then she said, "Night, please come down. It's safe now."

The light from the lamp across the street flickered and the bushes began to shake, but this time Nicole was ready for what was to come.

"Ahhh, looks like they're all gone. What a shame," David's voice came from behind her.

It might have helped that Nicole was so tired and in no mood to be scared that she was able to turn around and face David. She took a deep breath to help her stand her ground.

"Alison said I don't need to be afraid of you."

"She said what?!" David snarled.

"I'm not afraid of you," Nicole said as she walked over to the front porch and had a seat on the top step. "I'm not afraid of you, David."

"You only think you're not afraid. Well, look at me," David said with a wicked grin. He began with spiders and snakes, which Nicole calmly brushed away. Then David became a vampire, and then a witch. He even tried to become a vampire-witch, but Nicole realized that Alison was right. She didn't need to be afraid of the Dark.

Nicole clapped her hands and said, "That's a lovely trick, David. Are you finished?"

At that, David became back to normal. He grumbled, "I can scare you if I wanted to. Worse than any nightmare. But right now ---"

"Why are you here?" Nicole stopped him.

"Reason. Reason with me Nicole," David said.

"And why would I do that?"

"Do you know what they might have done if they ever caught her? They'd touch her all over with their fleshy hands."

"I'd never let them catch her," Nicole promised.

"Alison doesn't belong down here. She's Night, nothing more, nothing less. She can't keep coming down or else one moment there she is, and then the next, WHAM! No more Alison."

When David had said this, a small light arose from the palm of his hand. It fluttered for a moment, struggling to stay afloat before it faded into nothing.

"You're lying again, David," Nicole said with concern.

"Am I?" David said. And when he said it, he looked practically sincere.

Whether or not David was indeed lying or not, Nicole couldn't tell for sure nor did she have the time to put too much thought into it. One thing was for certain, Nicole noticed that Alison appeared to change ever so slightly each time she came down. It wasn't all in a bad way but she didn't appear to dazzle as much as she did like when Nicole met her the first time at the diner.

"Maybe she's becoming more like us," Nicole said to herself, trying to be hopeful. "She's probably adjusting to being down here."

However, Nicole did see Alison almost fall once or twice. Hopefully they were just accidents and not because she was getting weaker or feeling sick. Either way, Nicole felt it best not to take any chances. The following week would be the beginning of the second month since her first encounter with Alison. It was time, Nicole felt, to help Alison get into day. But how?

"That's a very thoughtful idea, Nicole," Auntie Ruth responded when Nicole told her about her plan. Nicole thought surely Auntie Ruth could think of something creative to do, with her being an artist and all. "Well, we could… Umm, I don't think that will work. How about if we… No. Why don't we try---" Auntie Ruth said as she grabbed a clump of her hair. "I'm sorry Nicole. I can't think of anything right now. Could I get back to you?"

Nothing like bringing Night into day has ever been done before, at least nothing Nicole was aware of. She wasn't upset with her aunt when she didn't even have one answer to give her but she knew somehow that something such as what she was trying to do was possible. There was one other person that might be able to help her. This person did make a mess of things after he first learned about Night, but he is the only one Nicole knew to have actually spoken with Alison. It was worth a try.

"Look, if you're here to chew me out about last night, I already got it," Ricky sighed. "I know, I'm a jerk. When my dad found out that I was part of it, he suddenly found all these chores for me to do." Ricky leaned down to pull another weed. He tossed it onto a small pile that he had started.

"Ricky, you've got to help me find a way for Alison to

stay down here all the time," Nicole said as she took a step closer to him.

"What? Oh no. I still haven't got this whole Night concept down yet. No, it's too much trouble," Ricky responded.

"I'm serious," Nicole told him.

"And what makes you think Alison wants to stay down here and be like us? You saw all that she could do."

"She told me. Alison says that she wants to see the sun. Would you want to live at nighttime all the time?"

It was almost 2:00 in the afternoon and the sun shone so brightly that it made any kind of work less appealing, especially pulling weeds. Ricky wiped the sweat from his forehead and said, "You know, I was thinking about taking a break anyway."

Asking for Ricky's help proved to be more useful to Nicole than she had originally thought. Was he smarter than Auntie Ruth or had better ideas? No. But what he did have were books. New books, used books, popular and rare books; about all kinds of topics. To be honest, it was mostly Ricky's father's books. His father collected hundreds of books throughout the years, not so much to read but because they looked nice on the shelves. It made Ricky's father feel like a college professor or some intellectual type when he walked amongst them.

"Well, here we are," Ricky said as he led Nicole down to the basement where the books were kept. It felt as if Nicole found a secret passageway to a different house, the kind that she'd only seen on television programs about rich people who spoke in English accents. The shelves, which there had to be at least seven of them, almost touched the ceiling and were lined with books.

"Wow! Ricky, how many books are here?" Nicole marveled.

Ricky shrugged his shoulders and walked between the shelves. Since the books were placed by how they looked, they were in no particular order, as in subject or type. Ricky started at a place he thought might be helpful.

"There are science books here. Astronomy. Hmmm, astronomy. Now that might work. Mathematics. We can find some kind of formula or something, and…"

A particular book had caught Ricky's eye.

"What is it Ricky?" Nicole asked with some anticipation.

"Just hold on, okay?" Ricky answered, pulling a book from the bottom shelf. The book revealed a picture of a muscular man in a shirt two sizes too small for him. This man looked very tan and had flowing hair. The sparkle in his eyes went with a smile of perfectly white teeth. The title of the book was, *Jim Lane's Ultimate Guide to Bodybuilding.* Ricky thumbed through the pages, forgetting for a moment that Nicole was there.

"Ricky, how is that supposed to help us?" Nicole questioned.

"Huh," Ricky muttered before looking up from the book. "We'll get to Alison stuff in a second. I promise." He was soon back to the book.

Nicole sighed but she too was soon captivated by the number of books in Ricky's basement. She made her way through the shelves in an attentive manner, pausing only briefly at times. What made her stop was when she noticed a small collection of fairytales on the second to the last shelf. Now Nicole had read many fairytales before and they were her favorite types of stories. She especially liked it when her father would read them to her. *Swan Lake* and *Beauty and the Beast* were her favorites. Fairytales were nothing new to Nicole but with her now trying to help Alison come into day, they had a new meaning. She was now part of a fairytale.

Nicole closed her eyes and when she did, she pictured her father and Alison waiting for the sun. Their eyes were full of love and courage. As the sun began to rise, Alison's body shook but Nicole's father was strong and he held her close. This made Alison stronger and soon they were both smiling because Alison had come into the day!

When Nicole opened her eyes, she hurried her way to find Ricky.

"Ricky, I think I got it!" Nicole said with enthusiasm.

"Got what?" Ricky spoke still looking at a book. This one was on cars.

"I figured out a way to get Alison into the day. We just have to get Daddy and Alison to fall in love again. And he can bring her to the sun," Nicole smiled.

"You were reading those fairytale books, weren't you?" Ricky asked with a laugh.

That's when Nicole gave Ricky a big slug on his arm. "Alright, alright. It could work," Ricky responded.

)))) ● ((((

Zenobia was the name given to the oldest part of the town that Auntie Ruth lived in. There were historic buildings (most of them were badly in need of some type of restoration). It also had its share of all-night stores, taverns and bars. This part of town had interesting sights to see but it also was known for its danger at night. Although most people would keep to themselves in Zenobia, there were certain corners where there were those only looking for trouble. This would seem a sort of place the David and the Dark would feel comfortable at but it was definitely not a setting for the likes of those such as nine-year-old girls.

"Stay close to me Nicole," Alison spoke in a quiet but with a stern voice.

To keep their comings and goings as safe as possible, Alison felt the two should move about Zenobia being invisible.

"This will help you know a little how Night sees the world," Alison said. "That's the thing with Night. We can be here, but at the same time we're not here."

"I think it's neat," Nicole responded. "It makes me feel like I'm a secret spy."

"People often appear and act differently when they think that there's nobody around looking at them," Alison added.

The two stopped at a street corner. They made sure they were far enough from the sidewalk to be in anybody's way. There Alison and Nicole watched as people would pass them. A small group went by joking and they were laughing. Another man, although he was by himself, was singing, while another was speaking louder than normal to his companions. A couple walked their way whom Nicole felt looked all too serious. She made funny faces at them as they came closer. She even did a little dance as they passed by.

"Are you sure they can't see me?" Nicole asked as she turned back to Alison.

"Right now they can't," Alison whispered. "But they can still hear you."

The man looked at the woman and said, "Did you say something?"

"What are you talking about," the woman responded.

"You said something like 'Do you see me?'" the man said.

"You're hearing things? I didn't say a thing," said the woman.

"Are you sure?"

The couple continued to argue even as they were a distance away. Alison motioned to Nicole that they were going the other direction. They passed a few more people before they reached the next block.

Across the street, at an outdoor patio of a corner tavern, sat Polly's mother. She was wearing a different dress but it looked similar to the one Nicole saw her wear the last time.

The patio was empty except for Polly's mother and man with thinning hair and a mustache. On the table were two bottles. The man lifted up one of the empty bottles and shook it. When he found that it was empty, he picked up the second bottle and poured the rest of the wine in it into her glass.

"That's Polly's mother!" Nicole said upon spotting her.

The man she was with stood up and excused himself before going inside. And when he left Polly's mother alone, that's when Nicole hurried across the street to the tavern. Alison called out after her.

"Nicole, don't…"

It was too late. Nicole had already reached the other side and was now close to the table where Polly's mother sat, sipping from her glass of wine.

"Shouldn't you be home with your children?" Nicole spoke.

This of course startled Polly's mother who once she heard Nicole, spit the wine out across the table. She dried her dress and looked around, appearing almost frantic.

"Who said that?" Polly's Mother asked, half afraid, half angry.

"Polly and George," Nicole said."Where's Polly and George?"

"They're, they're home. Where they belong. Night is not for children: it's for grownups," Polly's mother insisted.

Polly's mother looked under the table and behind her before speaking again, "That voice. I've heard it before. I know it! You're that obnoxious brat who tells lies. Come out where I can see you!"

There were other sounds in Zenobia that night, but Polly's mother saw no one around her. She examined the wine bottle and then her glass. She laughed, but pushed what was in front of her away.

"Ha! See? It's nothing," Polly's mother said as she nervously glanced back towards the tavern.

When Nicole took a step closer towards the table where Polly's mother sat, she began to throw the sugar packets in the air and pound the condiment bottles on the table.

"Wha --- what?" Polly's mother uttered as she had a grip on the table.

Slowly, Nicole raised up one of the wine bottles, and in her lowest, scariest voice, she spoke, "*This is what you get for not believing in Night. And... and being so mean. Boooo!*"

Polly's mother's eyes first widened before her head became wobbly. The man with thinning hair and a mustache had just stepped outside of the tavern when he witnessed Polly's mother faint. He rushed to the table to grab a glass of water and throw it on her face. Nicole stepped away from the table, and raised her hands up in victory. She had a satisfied grin when she turned around.

Alison was now a few feet away from her and was walking at a slow pace from the scene. She called out to Nicole. "Come on Nicole, it's time I got you home."

"But Alison," Nicole said as she walked at a brisk pace to catch up with her. "She was the one who ---"

The look Alison gave her wasn't the kind ones that Nicole was used to, but neither was it an angry one. Nicole wanted to know for sure.

"Are you mad at me, Alison?"

Alison shook her head and grabbed Nicole's hand as they walked along. They had walked another street before Nicole said,

"Daddy was in love with you."

"I know," Alison replied.

"Did you love him too?" Nicole asked.

Alison didn't answer immediately but it wasn't an uncomfortable pause for Nicole.

"I didn't think it was possible, us being together, so I wasn't sure how I felt," Alison began. "After he was put in the place where he is now, I went to see him several times. During the first few nights, I could see him looking out of his window. I was waiting, but he never called on Night. It was later that he stopped even looking out his window all together."

"I know he loves you still, Alison, I know it," Nicole said. "He just forgot. But now that I know you and others know you're real, he can remember again, and then you can see the sun."

"I'd like that Nicole," Alison responded. "If your father were to give me his heart, I'd be ready."

Nicole smiled when Alison said this. What also made her feel better is that she heard Auntie Ruth earlier making plans about them visiting her father. Things were coming together so nicely that Nicole wasn't thinking about all the work needed to make this happen. That would have to wait for another day. Right now she was happy she was with Alison, and it did give her another chance to be invisible.

Part II

The Crazy Man Who Believes in Night

PEAK VALLEY MENTAL HEALTH CENTER - Tuesday, September 2, 1992, 10:31 a.m.

The plan, although not official, was mostly straightforward. First, there was the matter of getting Daddy (Marc) to *believe*, not just pretend to *believe* because it felt good, but to truly believe in Night again. The second step involved him calling Night. The third step was much like the last step but in this case it was up to Alison to accept Marc's love, which barring any major unforeseen circumstances, she had promised to do so. The fourth and final step would be the most challenging; seemingly impossible in normal circumstances. It was a little tricky and maybe in need of a prayer or two, and for Nicole to keep her fingers crossed. This step meant that Alison would be able to see the sun, and then she, Marc and Alison would live happily ever after. This is more or less the way the plan was to go when Nicole thought it up.

"It's so good to see you Nicole," Marc smiled across a plain, wooden table, "I missed you."

"I missed you too Daddy!" Nicole responded.

"Now you said back there that you wanted to talk to me about something. What is it?"

Even with a painting of a blue and red sailboat across from her and a smaller one of a mountain scene and what surely looked like a comfortable cottage in the foreground, Nicole felt the room to be cold and uninviting. It felt as if they were being watched.

And they were being watched, and being listened to.

For on the other side of a two-way mirror, Dr. Judith sat and observed. Even in the dim light, Dr. Judith appeared to be a woman one shouldn't upset and would be wise to let her have her way. Her reddish-blonde hair was pulled back meticulously as her rectangular glasses lay halfway down her straight, pointy nose. Dr. Judith angrily typed away while she was listening to Marc and his daughter's conversation.

Nicole moved in closer to her father as she asked, "Daddy, will you tell me a story about Night and maybe... Alison?"

"Alison?" Marc responded with a raised eyebrow.

Nicole nodded with a smile.

"Now Nicole, Alison is just a character I made up, you know..."

"I know, but I like Alison and her story and I read all you wrote at least three times. Please, Daddy," Nicole pleaded.

For one to believe in something, it helps if they start thinking about it and talking about it as well. Marc could hardly refuse his daughter's request, especially since he hadn't seen her for what seemed to be such a long time. So he looked up at the ceiling and thought for a moment. And then, turning his eyes back to Nicole, began to tell her this story:

Alison follows the rules. She thinks they're important except when they don't make sense and keep her from being who she is. Alison is not the same as any other Night. Of course, I don't think I've met any other Night, but I'm sure, Alison is different.

There's this certain time of the year when Night has its' gathering. It's supposed to be an important time, so all of Night are expected to wear something dark. And then, here comes Alison, wearing this... dazzling red dress.

"I think I saw that one!" Nicole perked up as she spoke.

"What do you mean you saw that one, Nicole? You mean in your mind?" Marc wondered.

"No, I mean I saw that red dress before. Does it hang over like this?" Nicole remarked as she pulled her jacket down over her shoulder.

"Well, yeah. But..." Just then, something surprised Marc. His daughter began to describe not only the dress Alison wore but also what she looked like and the way she said things in such detail. How could Nicole know? Marc thought. Unless... Marc tried to push the thought away.

"Alison wore that dress when we went to see this nice lady named Mrs. Riley. She's old and she lives alone," Nicole continued. "Alison and ---"

"Nicole please, I beg you! Please don't," Marc stopped her. "I agreed to tell you another story because you said you liked them, but you can't keep thinking about it, telling other people like it really happened. Here, try this. It's something that Judith taught me." Marc pressed his fingers to his forehead and spoke rapidly. "It's just a story. It's just a story. It's just a story."

"But Alison IS real, Daddy."

"It could have been something I ate back then, yeah. Or

maybe it was because I was drinking. I didn't drink much, but I did drink. Whatever it was, I didn't have complete control over what I was thinking," Marc thought out loud.

"Daddy, Alison came down. She said she loves you now and she's been waiting for you all this time," Nicole went on.

"It's just that, I don't want you to end up like me, trapped in a place like this."

"Don't you believe me, Daddy?" Nicole asked.

From the dim lit room, Dr. Judith stood up with a sudden start. She had heard enough.

"This is not good!" she spoke aloud with disgust. "All my work and progress with Marc will not be ruined by this little girl!!"

Dr. Judith finished that last sentence in her report followed by two exclamation points. She exited the room she was in, leaving Marc and Nicole back to their conversation.

"Nicole, do you think I'm crazy?" Marc asked.

Nicole shook her head.

"Me neither. Now the trick is convincing them that I'm not. Judith feels I'm really close now. It's just ---"

"You, you remember Alison, don't you?" Nicole asked. "Didn't she mean anything to you?"

Marc pressed his fingers to his forehead and spoke, "It's just a story, a fairytale."

"It's not a fairytale when it's true. Daddy, you've got to call on Night so Alison can come down again. Please!" Nicole said clasping her hands together.

All the curtains in the windows of this office in the Mental Health Center were open. This let the sunshine in. Flowers and cute pictures decorated the room where a frail lady sat behind a desk. The plaque in front of her read: *Dorothy Collier - Doctor of Psychology.* Dr. Judith had joined her in the room. She pleaded her case.

"All communications with Marc Alexander must cease!" Dr. Judith demanded. "We can not have any further distractions."

"Are you referring to his darling daughter?" Dr. Dorothy asked.

"Beginning with his daughter!" Dr. Judith added.

"But she's just a little girl..."

"They're the most dangerous kind," grumbled Dr. Judith.

Not once during their visit had Marc promised his daughter that he would call Night down again. It began shortly after ten in the morning and lasted into the early afternoon. He did smile at Nicole when she asked him, but a smile can mean a number of things. At least her father stopped doing the silly trick that Dr. Judith had taught him after a while. The one that was supposed to make him stop believing in Night by simply putting his fingers to his forehead and repeating, It's just a story. When they left for that day, Nicole hoped that she had done enough to make Marc think about Night in the way he had before he was told that he was a loon.

"So this is how it's going to be?" Marc said out loud to himself as he sat up in bed, his eyes wide open. Something prevented him from sleeping that night. That something was mostly the subject matter Nicole and he had talked about a few hours earlier. Not only that, Auntie Ruth sat there as his daughter spoke about Night. Marc knew his half-sister was the silent type, but he thought she would at the very least have the decency to speak up if she believed Nicole was in anyway lying.

Then Alison came to his mind. Alison. Just saying her name made Marc smile. So he said it several times before he got up and out of his bed. He was starting to remember her face, her voice. It started out fuzzy and then...

"Oh no, not again," Marc declared. He recalled Dr. Judith and how much she had done to help him in his recovery. She warned him that falling back to these delusions may happen if he didn't stick to the program. He tried to do what Dr. Judith said but the thoughts about Night and Alison would not go away. Marc figured that the only way he was going to get any sleep was if he called on Night. Once he realized that nothing would happen, he'd know for certain that Night was never a real thing.

Marc cautiously approached the window. His heart was pounding as he hoped to get it over with as soon as possible. He looked up through his window into the night sky."I can't believe I'm doing this... Night would you please come down?" Marc said in a shaky voice.

A short amount of time would pass...

))) ❂●❂(((

"What is it Alison?" Nicole asked with a worried look on her face.

Alison felt something at the moment. It was so strong that it caused her to put her hand to her chest as though she was trying to clutch her heart. *Alison said she would give her heart to Daddy*, Nicole thought. *Maybe that's why this is happening to her.*

Alison's breathing had slowed down enough for her to answer Nicole."I'm alright Nicole. Please go on," Alison said as she had a seat on a bench.

As sometimes the case when calling on someone, it can be wrong time, for that someone may have already left. For Marc, he had just missed Alison, because his daughter had called on Night minutes prior to his attempt. Nicole wanted to see Alison to of course discuss how her day with her father went but also to see if Alison had any ideas to get him to call on Night. This meeting was only supposed to be a brief one. Nicole had no idea that her father would call so soon since it was still early in the night.

"...and then I helped Daddy put a jigsaw puzzle together," Nicole recanted.

"Those can be challenging," Alison responded.

"But every time I tried to talk about Night, he would just shake his head," Nicole said, shaking her head.

Alison's voice eased the girl's mind. "Your father looked very handsome the last time we were together. We danced and sang. He wanted to tell me something. I thought I knew what he was going to say, so I told him that it could wait. So now, we'll just have to wait a little longer, Nicole. Your father will remember Night again." Alison's attempts to appear hopeful were waning when she grabbed her chest again.

Nicole wanted to help her friend. She wasn't sure how to right now. The first day hadn't gone as well as she had planned it to go. Nicole was not about to give up now. She sat beside Alison and used her encouraging voice, "If Daddy doesn't call on Night this time. I'll try again tomorrow, Alison."

)))) ● ◖ ◖ ((

This would not be the night of Marc and Alison's reunion. Since Alison was not around when he called on Night, it was David who came down instead to visit him. This time he was sent with two others. Although they were also from the Dark, they weren't the same as he was. While David saw a purpose for each of his occasions to frighten, and it was almost an art form in the way he went about doing things, the two others, who will remain nameless, were just plain awful, not caring or thinking of what they did. It seems David's reputation had been damaged since it was discovered that he was unable to prevent a certain nine-year-old girl from calling on Night. The two who accompanied David were to make sure the job was done properly without any kind of mishaps again. This meant they would need to scare Marc enough to remove any thoughts of calling on Night again; thus keeping Alison from seeing the sun.

"Now just follow my lead," David instructed when they had reached the room Marc was being kept in. But one of the two pushed David aside and laughed a wicked laugh.

"Save some for me," the other one growled as he followed.

The walls that felt cramped to Marc already, appeared to be closing in on him as darkness filled the room and his mind.

"Let me outta here!" Marc screamed as he pounded on the door of his room.

In all the history of being scared, there may not have been anyone as scared as Marc was that night when the three from the Dark were finished.

))) ● ● ((((

Auntie Ruth and Nicole's return trip to the hospital that next day was amidst much confusion. They were made to wait far longer than usual with only the knowledge that all the hullabaloo involved Marc in some way.

"I'm sorry, ma'am. I was told that you have to wait, okay?" the receptionist told Auntie Ruth. "Can you wait over there please?"

Auntie Ruth and Nicole slowly backed up towards the direction that the receptionist had pointed towards.

"Here?" Auntie Ruth asked.

"No, there," the receptionist said as she motioned them to back up until they had reached the far wall. "Thank you."

A sign on the wall posted that the visiting hours were to begin at 9:30. It had been a while since it was 9:30. There was a television in the lobby with a cooking show on. A woman, who spoke with a bubbly voice, was demonstrating a Quick and Simple way of making stuffed peppers. There were also a number of magazines ranging from topics about sports to fashion. Plenty of things were available to help Nicole pass the time while they waited but she was too worried about her father to be bothered by any of those things right now.

"Auntie Ruth, they're not going to let us see Daddy..."

"Well we don't know that for sure yet, Nicole. Let's wait a few minutes and then ---"

The sound of rigid, hollow footsteps coming towards them had stopped Auntie Ruth from speaking any further. The footsteps sounded like they came from someone who was in charge and who wasn't all too happy. An annoying buzz announced that the door would be opened. From behind the door stepped Dr. Judith. One glance towards the receptionist made her move immediately. Without a smile, she summoned Auntie Ruth to the front desk. Although Auntie Ruth had motioned Nicole to remain where she was, Nicole instead grabbed a hold of her aunt's arm and followed after.

"Mizz Dowling. I'm Dr. Judith. Your brother Marc is one of my patients."

"Hello. How's Marc?" Auntie Ruth asked. "We were hoping that ---"

"The news is not good. I'm afraid to report that Marc's condition is as bad as I have ever seen in him."

"Why? He seemed just fine when we saw him yesterday..."

"Ahh yes. The key word here is seemed. A patient can give every indication that he's fully recovered when in fact that may be the furthest from the truth. There are a number of factors that are capable of reverting him back to a previous destructive behavior. Perhaps, your visit here ---"

"Are you blaming us?" Auntie Ruth responded with surprise.

"Not you per se. Not directly. But an experience from someone in his past can easily be the trigger to set off a patient. Whatever the reason might be, it's too early to determine what could have caused his behavior last night," Dr. Judith responded in a superior way.

All the while Dr. Judith was speaking, she never once looked Nicole's way. She believed that she could help her father but needed Dr. Judith to listen. "I bet it was the Dark. David was probably trying to scare Daddy."

The last words spoken by Nicole might as well have been spoken from miles away because it was as if Dr. Judith couldn't hear them.

"Oh, the months of research and effort. And then this. It's a very frustrating situation. But I assure your Mizz Dowling, that I am determined to find out what the root problem is with Marc."

"I told you. The Dark doesn't want Daddy to call down Night anymore so ---"

Dr. Judith could hear Nicole and she could not ignore the girl any longer. Her squinting eyes glared at Nicole and then to Auntie Ruth, directing her to see to the matter of controlling her niece. In an attempt to ease the situation, Auntie Ruth said, "Nicole, I think Dr. Judith is trying to explain why we can't see your father right now."

"I see now that I will have to intensify my treatment. Marc had shown significant improvements in the past weeks, but it's now evident that we hadn't taken his condition as seriously as needed. There are several approaches that I'm considering to ---"

"Dr. Judith, just tell my daddy that Alison will make sure it's safe for him to call down Night." Nicole expressed as she stood on her tippy toes.

"Enough!" Dr. Judith's voice almost sounded like a

shriek. "There MUST not be any further interruptions! Marc cannot have any contact outside the staff. Is that clear? Now please leave. I've already told him you've gone. It's for the best."

"I want to see my Daddy!" Nicole cried.

"Mizz Dowling!" Dr. Judith persisted.

"DADDY!" Nicole yelled, hoping her voice would reach beyond the door.

"Nicole, you can still write him letters," Auntie Ruth said as she put her arm around Nicole's shoulder. She looked back at Dr. Judith and asked, "She will be able to write her father letters, correct?"

"Yes, yes. Of course. Now please leave," Dr. Judith responded with a quick, almost forced smile before turning around.

)) 🌒 🌑 🌑 🌓 (((

Dear Daddy,

I am sorry you got scared by David. I know he scared me too once, but Alison said I needed to be strong if I should face David and the Dark again. And I wasn't afraid when Dark came again. So when you call on Night and if the Dark comes ---

Dr. Judith sat at her desk with the first of Nicole's letters. The look on her face as she read it was the one people give when they happen to be smelling something rotten. She hadn't even finished the letter before she folded it up and put it in the top drawer of her desk.

These Foolish Things

Days turned into weeks and Nicole still hadn't received any replies from the letters she sent to her father. Not even a little note that said, "I'll try to call on Night" or perhaps, "Thank you Nicole for the nice letter. Let me think about it." Even her times with Alison were noticeably fewer. As of late, they met usually only once a week. One week, Alison didn't come at all. Nicole tried not to be upset about it for she knew that Alison had chosen this strategy so she could save her strength.

Alison was also careful not to arouse any suspicions of too many visits to protect anything happening to Nicole like what happened to her father the last time he called on Night. Because they weren't able to be together as much, Nicole enjoyed her time with Alison even more.

Autumn was nearing its end so that meant the new school year was well underway. This kept Nicole's mind on more things besides Night. Although by now everyone knew that it was Kevin, Andrew's little brother, that had been the cause for the brouhaha that occurred at Auntie Ruth's front yard, Nicole had yet to deny that Night was real. This led many in Nicole's school to avoid her and sometimes tease her.

On the walls of Mrs. Penrose's fourth grade classroom hung pictures that the children made from last week's craft time. Since it was Autumn, Mrs. Penrose thought it would be appropriate if her class would draw and color a picture of trees changing colors. She also had the children paste leaves they found that had fallen onto their pictures to make them look more decorative. It was brought to the teacher's attention that someone had drawn two dark figures onto the picture Nicole had created. One was of a man who had vampire teeth with his tongue sticking out. The other was cross-eyed and had a squiggly mouth.

"Class, now who drew these awful men on Nicole's picture? Hmmm?" Mrs. Penrose asked while holding up the picture. "I'll count to three. One, two…"

Laughter broke out from the last row. The class turned to see three boys who were attempting to hide their guilt. The one with his head laying down on his desk was named Arthur. He was the class clown and the stripes on his untucked shirt weren't enough to hide the fact that he was a boy who very much enjoyed eating cakes and pizza.

"Arthur Brown," Mrs. Penrose said with a sigh.

Arthur slyly sat up and leaned back upon his chair before answering, "Who me?"

The other two boys continued to snicker as Mrs. Penrose held up Nicole's picture to Arthur.

"What's the meaning of this?" Mrs. Penrose demanded.

"It's those stupid Night people that Nicole talks about," Arthur sneered.

"They're not…" Nicole cried but turned forward before saying another word.

Karen spoke up, "If Nicole's picture is in the daytime, why did you draw those Night people there, huh?"

"Because…" Arthur stammered a bit before he responded, "Well, you're stupid. You probably believe in that Night stuff too."

"No I don't!" Karen said in return

The other two boys with Arthur snickered again. Before any more of the children could join in, Mrs. Penrose tapped her ruler on her desk.

"Now Arthur Brown," Mrs. Penrose began, "apologize to Nicole right now."

Arthur gave a smug look to his friends.

"Go on," the teacher persisted.

"I'm sorry for drawing those stupid Night people on Nicole's picture," Arthur responded grudgingly.

"Okay, now that's better," Mrs Penrose spoke. "Now open your books to page…"

Of all the days Nicole had spent at her new school, she couldn't recall wishing for the final bell to ring any sooner. And when it rang, Nicole gave a big sigh of relief but this day was not quite over yet. For as Nicole made her way with haste out of the front door, she heard,

"Hey, Nighty Night Nicole. Nighty Night Nicole!"

Nicole turned around to see Arthur and his friends jeering at her.

"That's not my name!" Nicole snapped back.

"Oh yeah? Why don't you prove it," Arthur returned as he stepped closer to her.

"Well, maybe I don't want to right now. Okay?" Nicole said as she turned back around.

"See, I told you guys," chuckled Arthur. And then he and his friends continued their silly chant, "Nighty Night

Nicole. Nighty Night Nicole."

Nicole rolled her eyes as she walked farther away from them. After a few steps more, she could hear Polly say to the boys,

"Why don't you leave her alone?"

"Why do you care anyway, Polly?" asked Arthur.

"Nicole's okay. She's a little strange, that's all," Polly said in reply.

That afternoon Nicole did not take the school bus home, which she had done for the past few weeks. It was understandable after the day Nicole just had for her to find her way back to Auntie Ruth's house another way, even if it was just for one day. Nicole had become familiar with several routes through her travels with Alison. They were paths that Nicole would dare not go alone at night, but during the day seemed safe enough.

The route Nicole had chosen was a little more than a mile away from the main road and then another three blocks to her destination. It ran by a ditch that was at least ten feet across at its widest point. She had noticed the babbling brook that had been there just two months ago had become nothing more than meagher trickle.

Almost at the midpoint of the pathway she was on, some people, most likely older kids, had pulled a fallen tree over the ditch to serve as a makeshift bridge to the otherside. This was the place where Nicole stopped. The night she and Alison walked this path, they had crossed this bridge. That moment came to her mind.

"There's a part in the Wizard of Oz book where the Tin Man chops this big tree and it goes over a ditch so Dorothy and her friends could cross over it," Nicole said that night as she cautiously walked across the fallen tree.

"Be careful Nicole. That log doesn't look too steady," Alison warned.

Nicole safely got across to the other side and made a small jump to the ground. She said, "I don't think that part was in the movie but this reminds me of that. C'mon Alison, now it's your turn."

She had almost forgotten how much grace Alison had when she moved. She looked as though she was a top gymnast from the Olympics when she crossed over the fallen tree to join Nicole.

This memory made Nicole smile and forget she was alone on her walk back from school. She hadn't gotten much farther on her way before something caught her eye. It was tiny, and was hidden beneath some dead leaves and mud but it shined enough from the reflection of the sun for her to see it. The other kids that had passed her earlier were now long gone and there didn't look like anyone else was coming soon, so Nicole crawled down into the ditch. Her shoes became a little muddied and scuffed as she made her way over to the object. After stepping over the thin trickle of water, she had reached it.

There was a familiarity about all of this as she bent over to take a closer look at what appeared to be some sort of jewelry. "Could it be?" Nicole said with excitement. When she picked it up, the object had revealed itself to be a bracelet. Nicole quickly splashed it in the little water from the ditch. She untucked the bottom of her shirt to wipe it off.

Once the bracelet had been cleaned enough, Nicole exclaimed, "It has to be!"

The bracelet looked as if it was very valuable and would cost a fortune. On the bottom was carved an exquisit A. Nicole remembered Alison showing it to her that night. The bracelet was very dear to Alison for it had been given to her by one of the older Nights. Nicole admired it greatly as well and when she asked Alison if she could see it again on another night, Alison frowned for she thought she had misplaced it, or even lost it. The bracelet was not lost, for there in Nicole's hand was Alison's bracelet. And it was not even four o'clock in the afternoon!

Dear Daddy,

Something really great happened to me on the way home from school. It has to do with Alison. When I was walking, I found something that was hers. It was day, Daddy, and it was Alison's bracelet! Alison hasn't seen it yet because she hasn't come down for a while but I know it's hers! She showed it to me one time. This means she might be able to see the sun!

I really need your help Daddy. Please write me back. I miss you and so does Alison. Oh, don't tell that Dr. Judith. She doesn't understand. She sounds like a screeching bird when she yells!

Dr. Judith had a scowl on her face as she wrote notes on the letter. On her desk was a folder that was labeled **Marc Alexander's Daughter - Letters**. She opened the folder and placed this letter on top of each and every letter that Nicole had written to her father.

To get someone not to believe in something is almost always easier than trying to get someone to believe in something, especially if that someone is grown up and should know better. Both cases can still be made more difficult when there doesn't appear to be any proof. Dr. Judith had no such proof that Night wasn't real. She had told Marc on numerous sessions that Night was just a story and it mostly made sense to him. Still, it was hard for Marc to believe that what happened to him involving Alison and the Dark was just something that he made up.

What Dr. Judith did have was --- time. Without any further distractions from Marc's nine-year-old daughter, she was able to proceed with her objective of intensifying his treatment. They would meet on a very regular basis, precisely at 10 o'clock in the morning, to keep Marc on the right track.

In her office, there were plaques and pictures displaying what a great psychiatrist she was. Naturally, Dr. Judith believed herself to be the best at what she did. But in all the time she had been in her profession, she had never encountered any case such as the one with Marc. If Dr. Judith was going to keep her reputation as the "best" psychiatrist, she knew she would have to cure Marc. She vowed not to rest until she accomplished her goal. This unfortunately meant that Marc would no longer believe in Night.

)))) ● ((((

On page fourteen in her father's journal are the words of a song he wrote about Night. It was a simple song but Nicole couldn't remember how the melody had gone since she heard it a long time ago. So she just said the words.

When you feel it in the Night
It's beautiful and bright
It's something you can't find in the day
When you're going home
You're never all alone
Night will help you find the way

After Nicole had spoken, she looked up into the sky and remained alone on the bench in Auntie Ruth's backyard. She had sat down there, waiting, like she did night after night. There were so many times that Nicole lost count. It had to be the longest time since she had seen Alison after calling on Night.

By her side, on the bench was her father's journal and a little box. It was rectangular in shape, the kind that one might find a less expensive necklace or some novelty trinkette. Nicole did make it look presentable by wrapping a bright red ribbon around it, which she had found in Auntie Ruth's studio.

With a half smile, Nicole closed her eyes. She just started to speak the words of her father's song when she heard Alison's voice singing the song.

When you feel it in the Night
It's beautiful and bright…

Nicole opened her eyes to see that Alison had now joined her. At this she lept off the bench and flew into Alison's arms. The child held onto her longer than she had held her before, and Alison understood. As she stroked Nicole's hair, Alison spoke up. "Thank you for waiting for me Nicole. I wanted to come much sooner but I've been assigned so many more tasks lately."

"That's okay, Alison. I'm just glad you're here now," Nicole said as she stepped back to look at her friend. "Will you be able to stay long?"

"I'll stay as long as you want me to tonight," Alison promised.

This made Nicole smile a full smile. While she was thinking of all the things she wanted to talk about, Alison noticed the little box on the bench.

"Did you get a present there, Nicole?" Alison asked.

Nicole turned and remembered the little box. As she picked it up from the bench, she said in an excited way, "It's for you Alison!"

"For me? What is it?"

"It's a surprise! Open it," Nicole said as she placed the little box in Alison's hand.

Alison gave a look of curiosity as she untied the bright red ribbon. And when she opened the box her mouth fell open. Alison asked, "Nicole, is this…"

Nicole nodded. She then went on to recount where and how she was able to obtain the bracelet Alison had lost. Alison thanked her and gave her a warm embrace.

"This is good, right Alison?" Nicole asked.

"Yes, that's right. This means a part of Night can remain in day," Alison responded. Her smile dimmed a little as she thought a little more about the situation. "Then again, it's just a bracelet. It's not me. It was an accident… but now we need your father to do his part."

"I wrote Daddy all these letters. He has to be planning something."

"It's hard for me to tell right now," Alison thought out loud. "Your father hasn't called on Night for quite a while and I haven't heard of the Dark making any visits to him since the last time."

"Daddy hasn't written any letters back to me," Nicole sighed.

Alison lifted up Nicole's chin. She said to the girl,

"Nicole, we mustn't give up hope. Hope often comes when we don't expect it." After taking the bracelet out of the box Nicole had given her, she put it around her wrist.

"Finding this bracelet is a very good sign Nicole."

Almost Dawn

The next morning after Alison's last visit would fall on a Sunday. Nicole found herself in a deep sleep so much that Auntie Ruth had to go up to her room to wake her up twice (almost three times) for her to get up for mass that morning. Nicole's time with Alison the night before had been so pleasant and fairly productive that when she did finally wake up, she was in a rather good mood. She didn't even mind that her eggs had gotten cold or that her toast became hard. She finished her breakfast promptly and was ready for the day.

During the opening hymn at mass, Nicole turned around and saw Polly and her brother along with their mother sitting at the pew across the aisle. Polly waved at Nicole and although Polly's mother didn't smile at her, it wasn't a frown either. She gave Nicole a polite nod before she continued to sing.

There was this feeling of hope that Nicole had since waking up that morning. It was the most hope she had felt in all the time she had known Alison. This carried onto the next day when she returned home from school.

"Nicole, can you come here please?" Auntie Ruth called out from the sitting room.

"I'm coming Auntie Ruth," Nicole replied after she had closed the front door.

The sitting room at Auntie Ruth's house was located next to the front room, which meant Nicole had reached her aunt in a short time. Upon entering the room, Nicole noticed a pile of letters on a coffee table. One letter was set aside from the rest and it had her name on it. Auntie Ruth smiled as she picked up the letter and handed it to her.

"This one's for you Nicole," Auntie Ruth said. "It's from your father."

Nicole had a seat and opened up the letter. The letter from her father read:

Dear Nicole,

I have a surprise for you. I think there was something you've been wanting me to do and with your mother gone, God rest her soul, I think now's the time. I want to make you happy. This is all I can tell you right now. You'll just have to wait until I get there.

I love you very much,
Daddy

Auntie Ruth waited for Nicole to set down the letter before she spoke up. "Isn't that great news, Nicole? The hospital informed me to expect him here shortly after three thirty on Wednesday afternoon."

"Wednesday?!" Nicole thought to herself. Yes she was happy to see her father and yes it was great news he was coming, but Wednesday? That was less than two days away! Nicole and Alison had prepared for the time when Marc would call on Night and try to help Alison into day; however, they expected that they would have been given a fair amount of warning to make sure everything was set in their plan. Even the letter Marc sent and its meaning just made things more unclear.

Her father's unexpected visit wasn't a disaster by any means but Nicole knew she would have to adjust the plan. Recently it had been difficult to know if or when Alison would make her visit but Nicole needed to speak with her as soon as possible. The only way she thought of doing this was to find a place where Alison would have no other choice than to come down when she called on Night. Nicole remembered the park where she and Alison had visited months ago.

"Night, please come down! I need to talk with you!" Nicole spoke in almost a shout.

Nicole waited. It was a moment or two but not long enough for her to feel it was time wasted.When Alison appeared to her she asked, "Nicole, what are you doing out here alone? It could be dangerous."

"I have to talk to you," Nicole responded.

"Yes, but it has to be the right time," Alison said. "It won't be long when it's found that I'm missing."

"Daddy's coming here the day after tomorrow!" Nicole returned.

"Oh," Alison responded. She wasn't as nearly surprised as Nicole thought she would be but it took her a while to respond with, "All right, Nicole. That's good."

Out of her pocket, Nicole pulled out the letter her father had written her and held it out for Alison to take. While Alison read it, Nicole spoke.

"I don't know why he doesn't say anything about Night."

"I noticed that too," Alison replied.

"I bet he's trying to use some kind of secret code just in case that Dr. Judith reads the letter."

Alison returned the letter to the girl.

"What do you think we should do, Alison?"

"Nicole, do you know what I'd like to do when I get to my first day?"

At this, Nicole's face brightened. She was giddy in her response.

"Uhmm. Go to the mall or something?"

Alison shook her head.

"Maybe a museum or, or maybe back to this park?" Nicole continued.

"You're getting close but you are not quite there," Alison replied.

"What? What? Tell me."

Alison looked up into the sky. When she had closed her eyes, she smiled. "I've thought about it a lot lately, of what I'd do. And then I came up with what would be a perfect day. I would like to just be in the sun, let it shine down over me. Long enough for me to know that it's real."

"Long enough to know it's for real." Nicole repeated.

"It would be you, me and your father."

"Oh good!" Nicole said.

"We'll just sit there for a while. We wouldn't have to worry because we'd have all day."

"That sounds nice, Alison."

"And then maybe we'll see about going to the mall."

The two laughed and savored the moment. There have been times with Alison that Nicole forgot Alison was Night but she would soon come back to the reality of who Alison was not soon after. But this time there was something new she felt. Right then, Alison seemed like someone she would meet during the day, perhaps for afternoon tea. This thought made her father's sudden arrival much more comforting.

The two began their discussion about how Nicole would bring her father to a certain area and he would call on Night and Alison would make her appearance. They had just about settled what they were to do and where they were to go when they saw something they had seen last time they were in this park. It was the sight of a policeman nearing them with a flashlight. This time, there were two of them.

One of the policemen shouted, "Hey, stay where you are!"

This is the part where Alison, in typical fashion, would normally have waved her hand in the air in front of Nicole and herself and then they would both appear invisible. But it wouldn't be the same result as the last time, for the two could still be seen.

The footsteps of the policemen were almost in rhythm as they got closer and closer.

"Alison, I think you should make us invisible!"

"I know, I'm trying Nicole."

Alison tried again and the result wasn't any different. The

policeman leading the chase called out, "I can see you!"

Realizing for the moment that her useful ability was not working, Alison grabbed a hold of Nicole's arm and pointed at a grove of trees.

"Over there," Alison directed as they ran.

Upon reaching the trees, they were able to find some suitable to hide behind. Nicole picked a tree about seven feet away from where Alison was. "It's okay for you to go back now. I think I can escape by myself," Nicole whispered. Alison nodded.

"Two nights from now when Daddy comes, it'll be okay," Nicole added.

"Two nights," Alison responded.

Since she was small, it was easier for Nicole to slip away. When she had reached a safe distance, she turned back to where Alison was. The police were at the tree where she had been hiding behind. They thought they had caught her, but Alison was no longer there.

$$))) \bullet \bullet \bullet ((($$

The following day was Tuesday, and for Nicole, it moved so rapidly that by the time she had gone to bed for the night she couldn't remember if it had been a good day or a bad day.

Now it was Wednesday. This was the day that her father was scheduled to arrive. This meant that Nicole had to take care of the matter of convincing her father that Alison was his one true love and not just imaginary. She hoped this would work so that Thursday would be the day that Alison would be able to see the sun. It was a lot to ask, even under normal circumstances. This plan took up so much of Nicole's thoughts that when Mrs. Penrose asked her the answer to a simple mathematical question, she responded with"Alison". This led to laughter from throughout the class. Nicole played along, saying she was only joking, and that the correct answer was actually 24.

"Very good, Nicole," Mrs. Penrose smiled but she gave it with a warning eye.

The bus ride home seemed longer than it normally did for someone like Nicole who was in a hurry. Once the bus had arrived at her stop, her watch showed 3:24. It wasn't too late, she thought, but she might not get there early enough to greet her father. When she turned onto the street where Auntie Ruth's house was, she saw one car soon followed by another pass the house but they did not make a stop. She didn't look at her watch again but Nicole was almost sure it had to be past 3:30 when she reached the front gate.

A car painted in a dark shade with dark windows approached the place she was standing. Nicole could feel her breathing quicken as the car window came down. A hand, followed by an arm and shoulder came out. Finally a head was seen. It was Nicole's father.

"Nicole!"

"Daddy!" Nicole responded as she dropped her backpack

on the ground.

The car made its stop directly in front of Auntie Ruth's house. Marc had gotten out just in time to catch Nicole's embrace.

"Daddy, I'm so glad you're here!" Nicole exclaimed.

"Hey Nicole, would you look at me? They say I'm okay now."

Nicole wasn't thinking about what "okay" meant when she looked at her father. What her thoughts were on now was when she was going to bring up the subject of Alison. Nicole hoped he would bring her up first when she heard the sound of the car door on the other side close in a firm, loud way. Her father stood up straight and Nicole turned to see Dr. Judith standing there.

"You remember Dr. Judith, don't you Nicole?" Marc asked.

Did Nicole remember Dr. Judith? Was she the one whose upper lip curled and eyes burned when she yelled at Nicole and told her she would not be able to see her father? Was she the one from that awful place where her father was kept all that time? Yes, she's the one, but only this time she was here in Auntie Ruth's front room enjoying a tall glass of water. Nicole could only count one time that Dr. Judith had even looked towards her while her father was speaking. It was like Dr. Judith was using some form of mind control, giving the words for Marc to say.

"So, you see, in order to stop these nightmares from occurring anymore, I had to transform my interior thoughts so I could take control of the energy I had. Thus, shining a light on exactly what it was I feared. That's when I realized that what I feared didn't exist," Marc explained as he looked back to Dr. Judith for approval. She nodded in assurance.

"And then... *voila!* No more nightmares!" Marc said.

"But Daddy, it wasn't Night that ---"

Dr. Judith placed her hand on Marc's shoulder and gave it a slight squeeze. He was quick to respond, "We... I, I think it's best that you don't talk about Night."

"But ---"

"Nicole, not one word, please," Marc said firmly to his daughter. Nicole opened her mouth to speak but no words would come out. Marc looked into her eyes and said, "Will you promise me this?"

She didn't want to answer. "Yes Daddy..." But it was all she could think of saying then.

"Good," Marc said with a relieved smile. Next he turned to Auntie Ruth and said. "That goes for you too, okay?"

Auntie Ruth held her tongue and simply responded with a shaky thumbs up.

"Now isn't this better? Things are going to be all right. I owe most of that to Judith. She really cared for me, believed in me. I don't think I'd be who I am today without her."

What happened next could have been a nightmare that David had brought but it was daytime and it was real. What happened next, Nicole's father, Marc, proclaimed as he put his arm around Dr. Judith, "That's why I asked Judith to marry me."

"What?" Nicole gasped.

"Really?" Auntie Ruth added.

"Yes," Dr. Judith spoke with her nose in the air.

"And she said 'yes,'" Mark returned. "This is the surprise I was talking about. I'm sorry I wanted to tell you earlier but we had to wait until Judith accepted the position at the University. And now she's no longer my doctor... but soon she will be my wife."

Dr. Judith held up her hand up for Auntie Ruth to see; the one with the ring on it. Nicole neither laughed nor cried when she heard the news of her father and Dr. Judith's plans. She stared forward with a face like someone who had just awoken and found herself in the middle of the ocean. Her father took the seat that was beside her and sat down. He spoke softly, trying to make her understand.

"...believe me, right now, I feel it's the best for me and for us of course. Judith is what we need, and once you get to know her, well... she's smart, yeah, and she's..."

))) ● ● ● (((

Later that afternoon, Nicole thought more about the surprise marriage and its possible unfortunate outcome. Maybe Dr. Judith wasn't nearly as bad as Nicole had imagined and she just needed time to get used to. And maybe, Nicole was being just a little bit selfish and should think about what's good for her father.

"Marc, why don't you try doing it the way I told you to?" Dr. Judith ordered as Marc was working on the computer.

No! Nicole thought to herself while she looked at the two. She couldn't believe that this not-so-nice woman was the one for her father. And what about poor, sweet Alison? She was so close to seeing the sun. Her father loves Alison and she him, at least this is what Nicole felt in her heart. What was to become of Alison? If only Nicole could let him know about Alison... but she couldn't. She had made a promise not to. She couldn't even write a letter. There has to be another way, she pondered. And then, Nicole smiled.

"Are you sure you know what you're going to say?" Nicole said to Ricky in a quiet voice.

"Yeah, yeah. Relax. I'll do it just like you said," Ricky responded.

Dr. Judith said she had some business to take care of and shouldn't be bothered. This would be a good time, Nicole thought, for her father to meet Ricky, the fourteen-year-old boy who lived next door. When they found her father, he was in the sitting room. Fearing that Nicole might be up to something, Dr. Judith didn't stray too far.

"Daddy, this is Ricky. He lives next door," Nicole said."He has something he wants to say to you."

Marc set the paper he had been reading down on the coffee table and looked up at Ricky. "So Ricky, what do you know?"

Ricky smiled and nodded his head for a few seconds

before Nicole elbowed him to speak. "Oh, Night is real. Alison is real. I've seen her and she's gorgeous…"

Marc sat up, his eyes filled with thought. Dr. Judith was standing at the doorway when Nicole whispered something to Ricky, and he added. "Yeah and you'd be a big idiot if you don't call her down ---"

Then with surprising speed and strength, Dr. Judith harshly grabbed a hold of Ricky's arm and ushered him to the front door.

"Hey!" Ricky protested.

"Out!" Dr. Judith shouted.

From the sitting room, Nicole and her father could hear the door slam. It was a bit awkward as they waited for Dr. Judith to return. She had just entered the room when a tap was heard at the window. They all turned to see Ricky standing on the other side. He yelled,

"Alison rules! Yeah!"

Like a flash, Dr. Judith was at the window. With a tight grip on each side, she pulled the curtains closed. Nicole whistled as she left the sitting room.

))) ● (((

It was nearing evening that day when Dr. Judith was discussing the wedding plans. Three months from the end of the week was the time when Marc and Dr. Judith were to be wed. Being the very organized person she was, Dr. Judith was almost done with the preparations. She had

Marc look over a small stack of schedules and lists. As they came to the end of the hallway nearing the front room, Dr. Judith pushed Marc, in a not subtle manner, into another room that appeared to be filled with old clocks, tables and chairs.

"Why don't you go in there and finish reading the plans I gave you?" Dr. Judith smiled.

"In here?" Marc asked.

"Please, dear. I thought you might be able to see them clearer in here. The lighting is better,``she answered. "I will join you momentarily."

After closing the door, Dr. Judith turned around to the rest of the house. On a shelf, plain as day, was the journal, *A Little Bit About Night*, which Nicole's father had written. And on the walls, hanging in various places, were some of Nicole's paintings of Night. There was a painting placed in such a prominent position that it would be nearly impossible for one not to see it once they entered the front room. It had two figures painted on it and they were holding hands. The figure on the left was labeled in big white letters **DADDY** while the other one had **ALISON** painted on top of it. There were arrows that pointed to the figures with a few hearts painted in the air between the two.

Dr. Judith had found a bag where she put Marc's journal in first followed by the pictures of Night that Nicole had painted. It should be obvious that getting Marc to think about Night again was not part of Dr. Judith's plans. But did these little episodes discourage her? No, far from it. Dr. Judith had years of study regarding the adolescent mind and was said to be an expert on the subject. She knew how they think and why they act in certain manners. Dr. Judith needed to show one particular child who was in control.

)))) ● ((((

It was nighttime and Auntie Ruth sat in her car with the engine running. Marc stood outside the passenger side with the door open. He was speaking to Dr. Judith who remained behind the gate in Auntie Ruth's front yard.

"Are you sure you don't want to come with us?"

"I think I'll pass this time. I'm still getting settled in," Dr. Judith responded.

Auntie Ruth had ordered dinner from Ernie's, a local restaurant with a menu that had a variety of dishes she thought her guests would enjoy. Her voice could be heard coming from the car as she called out to her brother,

"I'm sure our order is ready by now. You better get Nicole then."

Before Marc could reply, Dr. Judith spoke up.

"Oh let her stay. It'll give us a chance to talk and spend some time together. I want to try to understand her, and if we are to live in the same house ---"

"Good idea," Marc responded to the request. He got into the car, but before they left Marc added, "Tell Nicole we'll be right back."

"Yes, yes. Of course," Dr. Judith returned. "I'm sure Nicole and I will have much to talk about."

Once Dr. Judith's saw Marc wave goodbye and Auntie Ruth's car pull away, she turned and walked up the sidewalk toward the house. It was at that moment the front door flew open and Nicole stepped out. She hurried past Dr. Judith to the gate just in time to see Auntie Ruth's car turn the corner.

"Auntie Ruth and Daddy already left?" Nicole asked.

"It appears that way, doesn't it now?" Dr. Judith responded, her voice cold.

"Oh well, I guess I'll just wait for them inside," Nicole said. The smile she gave to Dr. Judith was a meek one but it was cordial. Nicole walked almost on her tippy toes towards Auntie Ruth's house. Although her attempt to remain unnoticed would have been noteworthy, she was not invisible to Dr. Judith who immediately took a step to block her path.

"What do you think you're doing?" Dr. Judith spoke in almost a growl.

Nicole stammered, "I --- I was ---"

"Well it's not going to work, you hear me?" Dr. Judith said as she leaned in closer to the girl. "You will not get the best of me."

Nicole thought of all the books she's read and movies she's seen about fairytales. She wondered if there was any villain in those stories like Dr. Judith. Of course the wicked stepmother from Cinderella came to her mind first... but

Dr. Judith was smarter than that stepmother because as was mentioned earlier, she had years of study in psychology. She told Nicole that her father listens to her and believes what she says is the truth. And that there was nothing that this child could do to stop the wedding, so she better behave or else…

"But my daddy doesn't love you. He loves Alison!" Nicole cried.

"Who's Alison? Can somebody please tell me who Alison is?" Dr. Judith asked as she shook her fists in the air.

"She's Night. She lives behind The Windows in the Sky," Nicole answered.

"Well then, show me this Alison. It's night now, isn't it? Where is she?"

"I have to call her down," Nicole said.

To prove that she was right and Nicole was wrong and that there was no such thing as Night or Alison, Dr. Judith said she would call on Night. She walked about Auntie Ruth's yard snapping her fingers one moment, whistling the next. Dr. Judith's laughter was a mocking cry as she held her hand up to cup her mouth, "Yoohoo… Night. Oh Night, where are you?"

Nicole observed Dr. Judith's outlandish display for a moment before she looked up at the sky and said, "Night, please come down. I need you."

Dr. Judith stopped when she heard Nicole speak. She turned around and asked, "Did you say something?" Nicole did not respond so Dr. Judith continued. "Oh, so you have nothing to say? Then have I made my point?"

Something happened right after Dr. Judith last spoke. It made the front light in Auntie Ruth's house go off.

"Okay Nicole, very funny. How did you do that?" Dr. Judith said. There was a slight tremble in her voice.

Just as sudden as the light had gone off, it was the same when the light had turned back on. And what the two that were in Auntie Ruth's front yard that night noticed when the lights came back on, was a pair of eyes floating in the air. They pierced the night and they were glaring at Dr. Judith.

"Wha --- what is that!?" Dr. Judith said in fright.

The eyes were soon followed by a twisted smile that could take one's breath away. When the whole body was revealed, Dr. Judith could see that it was someone from the Dark side of Night (which happened to be David). He spoke with a hiss, "Hello Judy!"

David knew what frightened her for she had been young once. With each step he moved towards her, he became *bigger* and *scarier*. Dr. Judith remained frozen where she stood. It was when David was right in front of her and whispered something in her ear that Dr. Judith fumbled for the keys that were in her pocket. She made a mad dash to her car and was quickly inside.

David had turned back to normal when Nicole went and stood near him at the gate. As they watched Dr. Judith's car speed off Nicole remarked, "That was cool."

"Well, it's just what I do," David replied casually as he

stretched out his arms.

"David, you made it okay for Alison to come down now."

"Shhhhh," David said, putting his finger to his lips but he did give her a wink.

When Nicole moved closer to him, David began to appear uncomfortable.

"Ohhh. You're not thinking about trying to hug me now, are you?" he said as his body shook.

Nicole smiled.

"Not tonight," David spoke as he moved into the shadows. "Perhaps we'll meet again Nicole."

David was soon gone, leaving Nicole standing alone for the moment.

Auntie Ruth's car arrived not much later. Before it came to a complete stop, Marc had opened the door and had gotten out. When he noticed that Dr. Judith's car was no longer there, he spoke to Auntie Ruth,

"See? I told you that was her!" And then he turned to Nicole who happened to still be standing by the gate "Nicole, where did Judith go?"

"She had to leave," Nicole answered. "I don't think she's coming back."

When Marc asked Dr. Judith to marry him, he hadn't put too much thought into it (meaning he didn't have much time to think if it would be a foolish idea or not.) But when she said "Yes" almost instantaneously, there was something about all of it that felt right to Marc. Now he couldn't believe that Dr. Judith was gone. Marc went driving in

Auntie Ruth's car trying to find her. Nicole was riding next to him as she described to her father what had happened to cause Dr. Judith rather hasty departure.

"...and then the Dark came down, like it did for when they scared you. Only this time, David came down by himself. He made this face and it really scared Dr. Judith."

"Ahhh Nicole, you shouldn't have done that to her," Marc sighed.

"I didn't do it!" Nicole protested. "She did it to herself."

"Here I am, I finally found someone who doesn't think I'm crazy. Someone I can walk with and hold again after all this time. She loves me for who I am."

"Daddy, Alison loves you. She loves you a lot more."

"Oh, that's nice Nicole, but you see, you can only go so far with people we make up," Marc said, turning towards his daughter. "Your daddy needs someone who's real. Besides that ---"

"Stop!" Nicole shouted.

There was a dog who had stopped in the middle of the road. It looked old and tired with the hair covering its eyes. Marc was able to slam on the brakes just in time. When the dog had scampered away, Marc pulled off to the side of the road. He came to the realization that he didn't know where he was going.

"I need time to think," Marc said as he turned off the engine. After getting out of the car, he stood in the middle of the road and looked down it. Nicole got out and joined him.

"I need to figure out what road she went down," Marc spoke.

"Can't you see, Daddy? Now that Dr. Judith is gone, you're free to love Alison."

"Maybe she went down that road. Nicole, where does that road go to?"

From where they had stopped, Nicole could see a place that was hidden from the road. She grabbed her father's hand and pulled him. "Daddy, come with me."

"Huh?" Marc was still befuddled from all that had happened that he offered little resistance when Nicole pulled him through some bushes and under a tree. A few feet more and Nicole walked no farther. The place they were was small but had enough space for what Nicole had hoped would happen.

"Daddy, you've gotta call down Night."

"Oh, alright, alright," Marc said as he looked up into the sky. "You know I'm only doing this because you asked. Not because ---"

"Daddy please."

After Marc called the first time, Alison did not come. Nicole thought her father's first attempt shouldn't count since he wasn't actually trying. She pleaded with him, "Alison said, 'If you want to be with someone, you have to mean it.'"

So Marc tried once more. Nicole was sure he meant it or at least looked like he did. And they waited for what should be considered a fair amount of time. But Alison did not come.

"Alison is not as strong as she was before, but I can tell that she's close. Try to remember," Nicole added, trying to sound hopeful.

Marc looked up in the sky once more, and this time when he called on Night, he spoke with purpose. This time, he did try. Nicole smiled because for the first time since her father left, she could see the magic back in his eyes. He did all that he could do to remember. And...

Moments passed, too many for Nicole. She could almost feel the seconds and minutes pass by. The night was so silent that she could hear her father breathe. Still there was no sign of Alison. When Nicole spoke again, it was a little louder than a whisper.

"C'mon Alison. C'mon Alison. I believe in you..."

Marc gave a breath of pity when he looked at his daughter. And then he shook the magic out of his eyes and said, "No, no... It wasn't real; it never was. I don't know why I'm doing this. I don't believe in Night anymore and look at me... I feel great."

"You can't stop believing in Night! It's because of what that Dr. Judith ---"

"That Dr. Judith is trying to reach out to you. She worries about you. She wants to help because she cares. Can't you see, Nicole? Judith wants you to be alright like me. So after we're married, she suggested some places where we can send you to..."

"No!" cried Nicole.

"It'll be just until you stop believing in Night."

Nicole could not listen anymore. Through the bushes and under the branches she ran. Her father called out for her. When he called the second time, he followed the way Nicole had gone but he could not keep up with her. And not finding her back at the car, Marc knew he had lost his daughter.

Nicole must have felt so tired when she made it back to Auntie Ruth's house for she barely had enough strength to open the front gate. Auntie Ruth's car was not there and neither was her father. Nicole eased her way unto the lawn and had a seat. She thought about all her father had said to her, saying that he didn't believe in Night. Nicole couldn't think of anything else she could do now to change that fact. And why didn't Alison come down? Did she forget, or even had second thoughts about coming into the sun? All these thoughts were making it hard for Nicole to even think at all. Was this the way this particular story about Night was to end?

"Poor girl," Auntie Ruth remarked when she found Nicole fast asleep on her front lawn. She picked her up and carried her inside the house.

))) ● (((

There's a routine Nicole does in the morning. It usually includes the following: getting up, brushing her hair and fixing her bed... This routine may vary depending on if she was going someplace special or had to wake up extra early. All and all this day seemed like just another day. But how could it be after what happened the night before?

The phone rang and when Auntie Ruth picked it up, Nicole heard her answer with a tone of surprise. "Why hello Dr. Judith. We were wondering what happened to you..."

Dr. Judith. Just hearing that name made Nicole's stomach turn. But now it looked like she'd have to get used to saying it. Nicole groaned as she got ready for school.

"No. I don't know where he is. I haven't seen him either since last night," Auntie Ruth said as she continued to speak on the phone.

Nicole wondered where she had placed her other shoe. She noticed that it was on the floor beneath the window. As she reached for her shoe, something had caught her attention outside the window. It couldn't be! It was well past dawn but could she believe her eyes? Out on the lawn were her father and a woman who looked like... Alison!

Nicole raced down the stairs and out the front door, She stopped right before the end of the porch and called out, "Alison?"

"Hello Nicole."

And then Alison looked up and let the sun shine on her.

The End of
the First Book